FIRE IN THE HEART

DANIELLE STEWART

RANDOM ACTS PUBLISHING

Copyright Credit Attribution:

Cover Design: Gin's Book Designs

Photo: Unsplash - Photographer: Philippe Wuyts

ISBN-13: 978-1973913009

ISBN-10: 1973913003

❀ Created with Vellum

FIRE IN THE HEART

Growing up on a Reservation in Arizona, Shayna always knew the day she left would be one to celebrate. Through hard work and careful planning she found her path out, but with it came a danger she could never have imagined.

Her brother Tao and her best friend Frankie pledge their loyalty to Shayna as she navigates the ghosts of her family's past and the near destruction of her future.

All with a little help from her second family back in Edenville.

CHAPTER 1

Shayna lived life with her fingers clutched to the handle of an imaginary escape hatch. Always formulating an ever-ready plan that lingered at the edges of her mind when things became difficult. Growing up on an impoverished Indian reservation meant there were constantly obstacles to overcome. No matter how challenging they became, there was always a sanctuary if she could make her way there. A place she'd be welcomed.

Life off the reservation had been both exciting and, at times, daunting. Envied by most friends for her deep, dark eyes, high cheekbones, and bronzed skin, Shayna was unquestionably and easily identified as Native American. Before she was anything else—a top scholar, an award-winning debater, the only person in her family to attend college—first she was Indian. It was the primary thing people noticed about her, commenting freely about her heritage as though it were an amusing novelty she was lucky to carry around. Just a vintage concert T-shirt from a long-forgotten band.

"How fun," her new roommate Chloe had announced, just moments after they'd both stumbled into their dorm freshman year, boxes still in hand. *"You're like a real Indian."*

The rest of the year had been filled with the same litany of foolish comments that came from a very sweet and naïve place.

She could hardly blame Chloe, a kindhearted Midwestern girl with lush blond curls and crystal blue eyes. Born into a legacy of some kind of condiment empire, Chloe had been ushered through life carefully. Like a new baby being driven home from the hospital at a snail's pace, the potholes were dodged, the challenges shrunk down to manageable dilemmas. Struggle was not in her vocabulary. Chloe was nice, but the common ground the two stood on was more of a tightrope than a solid surface. Most of the people she encountered at school were the same.

The stigmas, stereotypes, and folklore that followed Shayna after she ventured off the reservation did not start in a tiny dorm room. They were old and deep, and Chloe was not to blame. Being indigenous was like her shadow on an endlessly sunny day in the desert where she'd grown up, there was no getting rid of it.

Shayna didn't carry shame for who she was; there were days being different out in the world was exhausting. But she managed. Today, however, brought her to a different level of tired. As she stretched the ache out of her back, she practiced her smile. Knowing she'd need to camouflage the fear and sadness.

The people she'd soon face were not easily convinced by the blanket assertion that everything was *fine.* It would take more than that. She'd have to work hard to make it past all the emotional trip wires they'd set to try to snare the truth from her.

This part of the plan had to happen if any of this would work. The jingle of the bell above the door matched the nervous flutter in her heart. It sounded vaguely enchanted, and the warmth that spread across her chest as she entered The Wise Owl was equally magic. This restaurant was just an extension of the sanctuary she loved in Edenville, North Carolina. A long way from Arizona, but that also meant a long way from her problems.

"Take a seat anywhere dear," Betty announced with all the

warmth of a familiar love song. As usual, Betty's brown and gray streaked hair was pulled back into a bun and pinned properly into place. She hardly looked up from the counter as she finished the important job of adding gorgeous freshly baked pies to the display case. Shayna always admired how the woman she'd grown to love over the years was equal parts sharp and soft. Firm but fair. She balanced two pies on her arm as she spoke again. "We're as busy as a beehive in July right now, but someone will be right with you."

She was right, nearly every seat was taken during the lunch rush, and Shayna quietly opted for a stool at the bar. It was only another second or two before her anonymity was swallowed up by Betty's cackling laugh.

"Shayna girl, why didn't you say something? I'm sitting here treating you like just some regular old customer off the street." Betty did that familiar scolding but loving swat at the air as punishment for Shayna not speaking up.

"Hey," the man next to Shayna cut in with a wry smile, pretending he was insulted, "the rest of us regular old off-the-street customers take offense to that."

Betty was having none of it. "Oh Jeff, stop. You know I treat you like a regular. It's why I ignore you for the first twenty minutes you're here until you get frustrated and pour your own coffee. Now you," she said, pointing all her attention and her index finger back at Shayna, "how is it I didn't know you were coming to town? It's spring break right? Frankie is home from school tomorrow. But I didn't know you two had plans."

"We don't exactly have plans," Shayna fumbled and, like a doctor inching closer to a diagnosis, Betty's face lit with a knowing glow. She could already tell something was up.

"We love surprises," Betty offered, trying to put Shayna at ease. "Let me fix you up some lunch, and then we can talk more about it."

"I . . . uh," Shayna stuttered awkwardly. "I'm not sure if I'm staying. I was sort of passing through. I have a bus ticket for later tonight. I'm headed to the coast."

"Well, that seems like a later tonight kind of decision then, doesn't it? Right now sounds like a what kind of sandwich decision," Betty blurted out happily.

"Ham and cheese," Shayna conceded with a warm smile, in awe of Betty's navigation of the emotional landmines people set around themselves. At home there was never a moment to regroup. Take a breath. Just eat a sandwich and put life on hold.

"Coming right up. And you like lemonade right?" Betty asked, tapping her temple as though the old mind was still sharp.

"That's right," Shayna replied, the memory of Betty's fresh-squeezed lemonade making her mouth water.

Though the place was bustling with hungry patrons and the bell signaling meals were ready kept dinging, Betty never took her eyes off Shayna for more than a couple seconds. She ate her sandwich, drank her lemonade, accepted a piece of pie even though she was full, and then tried to insist on paying her bill.

"That might as well be a paperclip and two buttons," Betty said, pushing Shayna's money back toward her. "It's no good here."

"I never get a free meal," Jeff interjected with a joking pout.

Betty straightened her back and narrowed her eyes at him. "The fact we let you come in here smelling like a farm and looking like a zookeeper is the gift we give you," Betty scolded, and Shayna couldn't help but laugh.

Standing up and shuffling a little toward the door, she held her breath. She was counting on Betty's intuition right now. She needed this to go exactly as she had planned.

"Shayna," Betty called out. "You know, I had a girl call in sick today, and I'm so shorthanded. Do you think you could stay around a while and help get through the lunch rush? You know the drill. I always put you and Frankie to work when you visit. Everything is the same as last summer. We did move the butter up a shelf in the fridge, but I think you'll get right back into the swing of it."

"Of course," Shayna said, almost too enthusiastically to convince anyone it wasn't what she was secretly hoping for. "I'll grab an apron."

The afternoon rush morphed into a couple quiet stragglers, a few high school kids tapping on their laptop keyboards, and some eager older folks in for an early bird special.

"Come stay in our spare room tonight," Betty insisted as she slipped her apron over her head and folded it. There was no question in her voice. "Our house is simply too quiet. We'd love for you to have dinner with us and then you can head off in the morning. I'm sure the bus ticket is transferable."

"I am pretty tired," Shayna said, fighting a yawn. She hadn't slept well in weeks, her nights fraught with flashes of terrible images she couldn't erase. But she'd spent plenty of nights in Betty's house. Her entire high school career had been filled with traveling trips. The summers loaded with sleepovers at their place. Her best friend Frankie's family, the Coopers, had her along for almost all their family vacations too. These were good people, and Shayna was convinced if she'd ever get a restful night again it would be at Betty's house. "Are you sure I wouldn't be imposing? I show up out of the blue, and you're going to make up the spare room for me?"

"Blue, green, purple, I don't care what you show up out of, I told you long ago my door is always open to you. You have been a loyal and caring friend to my granddaughter for years. You are family. Clay is going to close up here tonight, so he'll meet us at home later. Come on." Betty slung an affectionate arm over Shayna's shoulder, and for some reason she felt the surge of tears assault her eyes. She'd been freefalling for days, feeling inches from the unforgiving pavement she'd inevitably collide with. Betty, with complete ease, had just pulled the ripcord Shayna had convinced herself didn't exist.

"Thanks, Betty," she mustered, swallowing back the emotion and resting her head on Betty's shoulder as they walked outside and toward the car.

"You have more bags than just that?" Betty asked, pointing to the oversized purse Shayna had hastily packed before running toward the bus stop in Arizona.

"I wanted to travel light." Shayna shrugged, adjusting the bag self-consciously.

"We can do a batch of laundry tonight. I'll pack you up a bunch of sandwiches, too, before you head to the bus in the morning. Maybe even some things that'll keep. Just like the good old days. I always loved when you showed up, ready to take on the world with Frankie. How many competitions did you guys win? Debate team. Spelling competitions. Mathematics. I was always so proud."

"You packed the best treats," Shayna remembered fondly. "You and your family did so much for me. I'll never be able to thank you all enough. I know there were plenty of trips my mother couldn't afford. Michael and Jules paid for so much."

"Money is a funny thing," Betty hummed as she put the car in reverse and backed out of the restaurant she owned. "When you really think about it, what is it?" She paused and Shayna realized the question was not rhetorical. She was waiting patiently for an answer.

"Money is power. It's what divides people. Lumps us together or rips us apart." Shayna knew her reply sounded ominously bad, but that had been her experience with money over the years. Or the lack of it.

"That's way more profound than I was thinking." Betty laughed, and the jolly tone made it impossible for Shayna not to smile. "Money is just paper and metal. It's just something we invented somewhere along the way. There are thousands of currencies outside of dollars and cents."

"I'm guessing you don't mean euros." Shayna giggled, trying to dodge the playful sideways glare from the driver's seat.

"Of course that's not what I mean." Betty hummed. "I'm talking about what you can add to a memory, an experience. I'm talking about the laughs you contribute. How much are they worth? The tears you dry when your friend's heart is broken. Is that twenty dollars? Two thousand? When you talk your dear friend into facing her fears. When you love without judgment. How do you measure that in dollars and cents?"

"I hear what you're saying," Shayna replied, not bothering to add the "but" she wanted to tack on. Betty would have cut her off anyway.

"My family has never thought twice about the value you have added to our lives. Every trip, every summer backyard fire, all the long car rides: you have paid your way with smiles, support, and kindness. There is no debt owed."

"I appreciate you saying that." Shayna sighed, tucking her long black hair behind her ears.

"Things like that are heavy," Betty continued, sounding unconvinced that Shayna was truly listening. "You pack them up on your back, carry them around, and don't even realize how they slump your shoulders over time. Your head starts to hang low and soon you forget how to hold yourself upright and proud. Why don't we leave it in this car?" Betty's eyes were wide like a grandmother presenting a plate of warm homemade cookies to her grandchildren.

"What?" Shayna asked, her brows knitting together. Betty was hard to follow sometimes. She'd preach in a way you couldn't help but love, but every now and then she slipped into a different language.

"Leave that weight right here. Leave the idea that you are less than, that you owe something to this family. You don't. Unpack it right in this backseat and forget it."

"All right," Shayna said through a breathy laugh, appeasing dear Betty. "It is pretty heavy."

"Shayna," Betty purred, wrapping her long warm fingers around Shayna's wrist and squeezing affectionately, "life is short. People say that so frequently that we all forget to believe them. I've blinked and here I am, all sage advice wrapped in wrinkly wrapping paper. Think of how lucky you are. You get the benefit of sound wisdom while still having that smooth complexion."

"I don't see any wrinkles at all on you, Betty," Shayna countered, patting Betty's creased hands that had spent a lifetime covered in flour or dish water.

Betty cackled and rolled her eyes. "See, that kind lie right there is my point exactly. That's got to be worth a million dollars."

CHAPTER 2

"A quiet dinner?" Shayna groaned with a huff as she counted the extra cars in the driveway and saw the commotion of people through the windows.

"Well, this is quiet by our standards. It's just you, me, Jules, Michael, Ian, Bobby, Piper, and their twins."

"So just everyone," Shayna said, the knot in her stomach tightened, not wanting to face the emotional interrogation that would absolutely ensue. "You know something's up." She sighed. "They'll be all over me."

Betty fanned herself like an old time actress faking innocence. "Little old me knows something's up with you? I thought everything was *just fine and dandy*."

"They'll see right through me," Shayna charged, sinking her head down.

Betty patted her shoulder. "True, this is the lions' den you're walking into. But these lions don't want to eat you, they just want to circle around and protect you from whatever you're running from."

"I'm leaving in the morning," Shayna reminded her as they stepped out of the car, and the familiar sound of what Shayna liked to call "laugh-fights" spilled from the house. The combination of fervent debate and silly personal attacks created verbal fireworks. Conversations would rise and fall, like the rain turning from drizzle to a downpour then fading back again. These people, who she'd been absorbed into like water in a sponge, were wholly unique. And she loved them, though she didn't love the idea of facing them right now.

"Shayna," Jules said, nearly shrieking at the surprise. Her long bright red hair was pulled back into a ponytail, and she looked as chic as ever. Her dear friend, Frankie, always gave her mother a hard time, but Shayna thought Jules was perfect. "What in the world are you doing here?" There was a buzz of commotion that filled Shayna's ears and made her head spin. The hugs she was bombarded with were welcomed and were maybe the only thing keeping her on her feet. It felt good to be back in the arms of people who knew her heart, even if she was trying to hide it right now.

"I'm just passing through and couldn't miss dinner. Betty's cooking is worth a little layover." Shayna could feel the heat of everyone's eyes on her. She was not passing the lie detector test, but they all kindly allowed her some grace. They'd interrogate her, but they'd feed her first.

"Come in," Michael said, his salt and pepper hair and bright smile always perfectly matched with his kindness and charm. The quintessential dad. Of all the things Shayna coveted over the years, Michael's parenting was the top of the list. With him the boundaries were fair and clear. Freedoms earned and respected. So many times Frankie would complain about her parents, and Shayna would just roll her eyes and remind her how good she had it. Shayna had grown up without a dad, and the hole it left in her life was enough to swallow her up sometimes. "It's been months since we've seen you. How are things?" Michael pressed, his eyes focused in on her, searching for a sign something might be wrong.

"The last time I heard from your mother," Jules interrupted, practically shoving her husband aside and ushering Shayna to a seat by her at the table, "she told me you were third in your class at university. You must be working your butt off. I hope you're having fun too. It's your junior year; you're settling in nicely?"

"Nice enough," Shayna shrugged, and it pained her to lie to them. "Everyone is friendly."

"Everyone is friendly or you've made friends?" Piper asked, looking worried as she started passing some food around.

"It's strange," Shayna sighed, ready to speak some truth she'd been burying for a while. If anyone would understand, it would be them. "I spent all my time trying to get off the reservation. I put my grades first. I told Tao to stop bothering me about how I was selling out my people. Now that I'm out in the world, I realize I can go a whole week, a whole month, without ever seeing someone who looks like me. Or someone who knows anything about the quilts of our grandmothers or the desert dreams of our grandfathers. The closest I got was a Halloween party where an entire sorority dressed up as sexy Indians."

"Distasteful," Betty hummed. "I've just finished reading an article about that. It's called cultural appropriation. Did you know that?"

"I've heard the term." Shayna smirked. "But really it's not a big deal. It's just interesting. That's all. Different than I thought it would be."

"Do you have a chance to get back to the reservation often?" Michael asked, clearing his throat and attempting to look completely unconcerned about this surprise visit.

"I've been meeting my mother at the hospital and staying there with her while she gets chemo. It's a long trip, and normally I have to get back to school right after. Her treatment center is off reservation, so I haven't really been back to the reservation since last summer."

"How is she doing?" Betty asked, raising the cross necklace from her chest and kissing it as she whispered a prayer. "She's on my mind often."

"She's hanging in there," Shayna reported, trying to force some optimism onto her face. "And she appreciates your kind words. She's been getting your letters. They mean a lot to her."

"And Tao?" Jules asked, the pitch of her voice too sharp to sound natural. She let the question hang out for anyone to pluck it from the air and add context.

Piper jumped in. They were always a good team in these moments. "We so enjoyed your last visit. Your brother made quite the impression on the family. Yet Frankie doesn't seem to want to spill the beans on whether or not there is anything going on between them. Are they an item finally?"

"They're both being pretty tight-lipped about it," Shayna grinned, thinking fondly of the blossoming relationship between her best friend and her brother. While most people would have squirmed at the idea of those worlds colliding, Shayna had seen how their bond made each of them better versions of themselves. "I know they've visited each other a few times this year. Frankie helped Tao get his GED, and he's on track to enroll for online college classes soon. He's not willing to leave the reservation yet, but he's made some impressive progress on issues there. People are saying he could end up being a leader someday and make real change for the community."

"And he's helped her a lot," Michael interjected, looking torn by having to compliment the guy in his daughter's life. "He has a great attitude, and I can hear his impact on Frankie when we talk now. They're a good pair. If they're a pair, that is."

"I wish I had more to tell you," Shayna apologized. "I've been so busy at school I haven't been getting the latest gossip. All I can tell you is they both seem really happy when I check in."

"You'll be able to see Frankie tomorrow," Jules said, laying her napkin across her lap. "Does she know you're here?"

"No," Shayna said quickly. "I'll be gone in the morning before she gets in. I have to catch the bus."

"Where is it you're going?" Bobby asked, and suddenly he seemed more like his cop self than the friendly uncle of her best friend.

"The beach," Shayna explained. "Do you remember that science competition we went to on the coast in tenth grade?" she asked Michael, her chest warming with the fond memories. "That was the first time I'd ever seen the ocean. I want to go back there. Feel that feeling again."

"Sounds like you're on some kind of journey," Betty said, the words dancing the line between statement and question. "Why is it you have to do that alone?"

"Yeah," Jules said, lighting with excitement. "Maybe we can all go down. We have the whole week with Frankie, and we weren't sure how we were going to spend it. The beach could be fun."

"No," Shayna shot back. "I want to go alone. Maybe I should head out tonight. I appreciate everything you are trying to do here, but I just want to be alone."

"Tell us what's going on, Shayna," Bobby said, his dark eyes raking over her face. "We've known you long enough to tell something is up. You can trust us. Whatever it is, we can help."

"A lawyer and a cop are about the last people I should talk to right now." She pushed her chair back from the cramped table and rushed out of the room. Just as she pushed the squeaking screen door open two headlights cut down the dark driveway.

"Who's that?" Michael asked, the first one on her heels. "Is that a cab?

"Looks like it," Bobby said, instinctively stepping in front of Shayna, who was now frozen with fear.

"Oh no," she said, pressing her hand to her forehead as she watched Nicholas step out of the car and pay the driver. His long shaggy yellow hair caught the moonlight, and she could see a look of bewilderment in his eyes.

"Who is he?" Bobby asked, turning halfway to direct his question at Shayna, but never taking his eyes off the approaching man.

"Shayna," Nicholas said, looking relieved as he jogged to close the gap between them while the cab pulled out of the driveway. Without the bright headlights, the night seemed to close in around them.

"Whoa," both Michael and Bobby said, each slamming a hand onto his chest and backing him down the porch steps awkwardly. Jules, Betty, and Piper spilled out onto the dimly lit porch, and Shayna could see they were like coiled springs pressed down tight, ready to burst up if the moment called for it. "Who are you?" Bobby asked, his deep voice laced with intimidation.

"My name is Nicholas, and I'm here to get Shayna," he said, as though the simple answer would have them moving to the side. But they did not budge. Nicholas had no idea what he was up against right now.

"She's not going anywhere," Michael asserted. "Why don't we call that cab back? You start walking, and it can pick you up on the road."

"Why?" Nicholas asked. "Listen, there is some kind of confusion here. I'm Shayna's friend, and we have to go. Shayna," he said, looking through the small gap between Michael and Bobby's' shoulders, imploring her to speak up. But she couldn't. Words were like bubbles popping in her throat before she could let them out. "You know we need to leave. You can't stay here. These people can't help you."

"You know what?" Jules interrupted, bumping her way to Michael's side. "You don't know a damn thing. This is private property. I say we count to ten and then settle this trespassing the southern way."

"Lady," Nicholas said, twisting his face up in confusion, "calm down."

"Oh man," Bobby said with a huff. "You must be dumber than you look. You don't tell a redhead to calm down, and you certainly don't go calling her *lady*."

"She's Jules," Nicholas noted calmly. "Then Piper, Betty, Michael, and Bobby." He pointed at each of them and got their names correct. "Shayna's told me everything about you guys, and I knew she'd turn up here if she was in trouble."

"What kind of trouble are you giving her exactly?" Betty asked, propping a hand up on her hip and eyeing him angrily.

"I'm not giving her any trouble. Shayna, please tell them I'm not the problem here. We need to go. They can't protect you." He tried to move past Bobby and Michael, which was just slightly stupider then telling Jules to calm down.

"You know what," Michael said, grabbing one of his arms as Bobby quickly grabbed the other. The two men lifted Nicholas off his feet and backed him up a yard from the house. "I think Jules might be right. Trespassers aren't welcomed here."

"You're a cop," Nicholas protested. "You can't throw me out of here like this. You can't put your hands on me if I'm not doing anything wrong."

"You see my badge?" Bobby asked, shoving Nicholas backward. "Because right now I'm just a guy who wants you to beat it. If you don't, I plan to make you."

"Wait," Shayna finally said, stepping forward. "He's not the problem. He thinks he's here to help. It's all right. Don't hurt him."

"If I tracked you down," Nicholas called out over Michael's shoulder, "they will too. We need to go now. They'll find you."

"In the house now," Betty finally ordered. "Every single one of you. We don't need to be airing our business out here into the night. But you," she said as they began to file in and Nicholas was within threatening finger-pointing distance, "you don't get any dessert."

"Okay," Nicholas shrugged, as if her punishment was ridiculous.

"You don't know how big of a deal that is yet," Bobby grunted. "But you will."

CHAPTER 3

Betty had moved the kids to their tent in the backyard, equipped with flashlights and jars for catching fireflies. Now it was time to get down to the heart of the matter.

"I want the truth," Michael boomed paternally. "You aren't going anywhere, so you can stop making that case."

Nicholas huffed the way only a half man, half child can. "They can't help you, Shayna. They have obligations because of their jobs, and they have to do what's required of them. Just because they like you—"

"First off," Shayna cut in quickly, "you don't know them at all. If anyone in the world can help, it's these people in this room. It doesn't matter what their jobs are. Loyalty means more to them than anything."

"Sing it, girl," Betty said in a breathy whisper as she glared at Nicholas.

"We can help," Bobby assured her. "No matter what it is, Shayna. Just tell us so we can figure out what to do."

"I can't tell you everything." Shayna sighed in defeat. "I don't want to bring the same trouble down on you that I've gotten myself into. There are some powerful people I've crossed, and they're not going to stop until they silence me."

"Silence you?" Bobby asked. "What do you mean by that?" There was a grave seriousness in his voice, and Shayna found it oddly comforting. They knew her well enough to be alarmed. To believe her.

"I don't know," Shayna said, heat rolling over her body as she tried to find the line she wouldn't cross. What would she tell them? What would she hold back? How much could they actually help, or would they get dragged into the vortex that was already pulling her toward oblivion? "The only thing I know is I have to leave. They've made it clear they want me gone."

"How?" Betty asked, sliding a large mug of hot chocolate with whipped cream over to her. Shayna had long since graduated to coffee, but this place was a time warp. When you came back it was all: *If you take a soda make sure you finish the whole can; don't waste it. Call me when you get there. Put your sweater on so you don't catch a chill.* There was no outgrowing the need for the weird cocktail of worry mixed with love.

Shayna took the large mug of cocoa and sipped from it. The perfect temperature. Safely cooled before it was handed to her. "My scholarships have been revoked. I can't go back to school. My mother had been accepted to a clinical trial. It was something she qualified for through the reservation and would be an enormous improvement to any kind of treatment she could otherwise afford. She's since been dropped from it. I know they wanted to threaten Tao but can't really touch him. He's insulated himself on the reservation over the years, and it's one of the few places they don't have power."

"Who?" Piper asked, and Shayna watched her hands ball into a fist. Frankie had spent many nights on the phone with Shayna over the years, spilling everyone's story. Piper had a fire in her when it came to injustice, and Shayna's words were stoking it to life.

"It doesn't matter," Shayna dismissed, slumping back in her chair. "They have the power. I was warned and I persisted. I need to get them off my trail for a while. They need to think I've disappeared."

"Disappeared?" Jules scoffed. "You're just going to grab a hobo stick, tie a handkerchief to it, and ride the rails? Warm yourself by a trashcan fire? That sounds like you've given it a lot of thought."

"I'll be fine on my own," Shayna protested. "I've always been."

"Maybe you've been fine," Betty corrected, "but you've never been alone. And you aren't now. All power has its limits, and I'll tell you what, my doorstep is usually a pretty good limit."

"Another car," Bobby said, raising one hand in the air to quiet them all as the sound of an engine could be heard approaching. "You expecting anyone else?"

"No one good." Shayna gulped.

"Go upstairs," Betty said, shooing both Shayna and Nicholas toward the staircase. "To the attic door in my bedroom closet. Stay put until we come get you."

Shayna pulled Nicholas along and drew in a deep breath as she entered Betty's closet. The silky soft sleeves of all her dresses and shirts brushed against Shayna's hair as they ducked below the clothes and popped up on the other side. A journey she'd taken many times before with Frankie on cool fall evenings. A tiny door with a set of narrow stairs was all that stood between them and the best hide-and-go-seek spot Shayna had ever used.

"Come on, we can see out the front of the house through the small porthole," she explained as Nicholas turned his broad shoulders sideways to get up the stairs.

"It's him," Nicholas whispered, as they positioned themselves by the small window and looked at the group who had now moved onto the front lawn to greet the latest arrival.

Shayna shushed him. "I want to hear what he's saying. This is going to be bad." She lifted the latch and quietly pushed the port-hole open a little.

"Can I help you?" Michael asked, strolling up to the man. "We don't get many unexpected guests this late at night around here."

"Sorry to be a bother," the man apologized, tipping his chin as a hello. "My name is Sheriff Lyle Dobbins. I've been traveling all day, so you'll have to excuse the wrinkles." He patted at his half tucked-in, button-up shirt and rumpled khakis.

"Sheriff?" Bobby asked, straightening up a bit. "From where?"

"Sun Mountain, Arizona." Lyle watched all their faces for some kind of reaction, but he didn't seem to get anything. He didn't realize, as Shayna did, these people were pros.

"That's a long trip," Betty replied flatly. "But this isn't a bed and breakfast. One of the boys here can point you in the direction of a place in town to stay."

"I have some accommodations," Lyle corrected, folding his arms across his wide chest. "I'm actually here on business, unfor-tunately. I'm looking for a girl who has some outstanding warrants. Intel said she has friends in this town, and she might likely seek refuge here. Apparently she's visited you many times before." He pulled a folded paper from his breast pocket and handed it to Michael. She already knew what it was. Her face on a wanted poster. She'd seen it handed around on campus before she took off.

"There must be some kind of mistake," Michael said, quickly refolding the paper and shoving it back to Lyle. "Shayna is no criminal. It's laughable, actually."

"You know who isn't laughing?" Lyle cut in, tucking the

paper away. "The man she assaulted who spent a week in the hospital."

"That's the charge?" Piper asked. "Assault?"

"One of the charges. She's also wanted for breaking and entering, destruction of private property, and burglary. Now I'm hoping you kind folks will do the right thing and tell me where she is."

"Not here," Betty said, shrugging her shoulders. "I'm not sure where she is."

"Your intel was wrong," Jules agreed. "We haven't seen Shayna since last summer. Now I suggest you look a little deeper into whatever case you have against her, because I'd bet on my mother's life she's not guilty of assaulting anyone."

"If you're her mother," Lyle began as he nodded over to Betty, "you may want to ask her to bet on something else. Here." Pulling his phone out, he clicked a few buttons and handed it over. Shayna knew what those photographs would be as well. The still frame shots that showed her knocking down Emanuel Overton. He took a fall that broke two vertebrae in his back. Obviously the still pictures didn't tell the whole story, but they painted her guilty.

Lyle continued in the worst way possible: smugly. There would be no tolerance for that here. "There's a little thing called obstruction of justice. I could throw you all in jail for withholding information."

"Want my cuffs?" Bobby asked coolly. "I can run in the house and grab them and my badge. I can even give you a ride into the precinct, though my shift doesn't start until tomorrow."

"You're a cop?" Lyle asked, clearing his throat. "Well then, you know something about obstructing justice and the consequences."

"I do," Bobby nodded, then gestured over toward Michael. "Not nearly as much as Michael here, you know being a lawyer and all. He's very familiar with things like intimidation and over-reaching of powers by the police. We usually leave all the legal mumbo-jumbo to him."

Even from her vantage point Shayna could see Lyle's face fall slightly. A small victory, but she wasn't naïve enough to believe it would last long.

Michael capitalized on the momentum. "I, along with everyone here, would be happy to attest to the kind of young lady Shayna is. Whatever the circumstances, I would stake my career that they can be explained away."

Shayna felt her stomach churn, because she knew how wrong Michael was. They should all stop betting on her. Maybe the circumstances warranted her behavior, but it didn't mean they didn't happen. You could be *right* and *guilty* all at once.

"As a man of the law you should know it's facts that convict someone, not sentiments," Lyle grunted as he yanked on his sagging belt. "Now, I understand that this girl is some kind of friend of yours—"

Betty cut him off. "She's family," she corrected curtly.

"Doubt that," Lyle scoffed, looping his fingers into his belt and arching his back as he chuckled. "She's not your family. Not by the looks of any of you. Not enough red skin around here for me to believe that."

Jaws dropped open and eyes widened in disbelief. Even if they were rattled by the remark, Shayna knew it would not go unanswered.

"Not one more word," Betty ordered, gesturing with her hands for him to be silent. "Your lips do not open one more time while standing on my property." When he shifted his mouth and furrowed his brows, looking like he might speak, she jumped in. "Uh, no. I mean it. Close your mouth, get in that car, and drive off my property. Come back with a search warrant and some view-points that have evolved further than a caveman, and I'll consider talking with you again. Until then, scat." She motioned like she was chasing a raccoon from her garbage and charged at him. "Go on."

"Is she serious?" Lyle asked as he raced toward his car, stumbling slightly over his own feet.

Jules moved forward to encourage him. "As serious as a hungry monkey in a banana tree. You best head out. There's nothing here for you but trouble."

"I'm an officer of the law," Lyle said as he fell clumsily into the front seat of his car. "I'm here on official—"

"If we have anything we need to tell you, I'm sure we can get in touch," Michael said,

guiding Jules back, doing this man a great favor by saving him from her wrath. Lyle dropped the flyer with Shayna's face on it onto the driveway and didn't bother slowing down to pick it up. Like a tiny gang, united in every movement, they all offered Lyle a glimpse of their backs as they moved toward the house.

Nicholas sighed loudly with relief as he leaned his head against the dusty window frame and closed his eyes. "They lied for you. I never would have thought they'd actually obstruct justice for you."

"In their eyes, they weren't obstructing justice. They were upholding it," Shayna corrected. "Because they know the real meaning of justice. But don't look so relieved. Lyle won't give up, and that's not our biggest problem anymore."

"What's our biggest problem?" Nicholas asked, furrowing his brows together and looking worried. Shayna couldn't blame him. In his mind, warrants for her arrest and a cop hell-bent on arresting her would be as bad as it gets.

"It's coming up those stairs right now," Shayna said, standing and drawing in a deep breath as though she were readying for a fight. There were too many stomping footsteps and intertwined words to tell who'd be coming through the attic door first. It didn't really matter what order they spilled in, Shayna knew the stakes had just been raised.

"I think we could jump out this window," Nicholas said, with a little snicker, trying unsuccessfully to lighten the moment.

"I thought of that," Shayna replied utterly defeated. "It doesn't open wide enough."

"Shayna," Betty's voice bellowed as she elbowed her way through the small door and into the dim attic. "I figure a warrant for your arrest and me chasing a cop off my lawn earns me a little bit of explanation. You agree?"

"Yes ma'am," Shayna said with a gulp.

"Downstairs," Michael demanded sternly as everyone shuffled their way out of the now crowded attic. "It's too damn cramped up here for me to yell the way I want to."

Piper hung back; staying by Shayna's side, she leaned in. "That window doesn't open wide enough to jump out of does it?"

"Nope," Shayna sighed, hanging her head low. "It's time to face the music."

"Don't worry too much," Piper said, nudging her with a playful elbow. "It's a familiar tune. It used to be my favorite song."

CHAPTER 4

"You obviously didn't assault anyone," Michael asserted, a breathy and defeated laugh on his turned down lips. "So why is that guy waving this paper around. Is he even a cop?"

"He is," Nicholas said, tentatively interjected. "I've known him most of my life. He won't give up until he gets what he came for."

"And I did assault someone," Shayna corrected, her hands half covering her face. "Not on purpose, but those charges against me are technically true."

"Technically," Betty hummed, waggling her brows up and down in disbelief. "Like the way Piper can technically cook, even though we all ask her not to? Explain *technically*."

"I broke into a facility owned by the Hillderstaff family. I was trying to find some documents I needed. It was wrong, but I was doing it for a good reason." Shayna could feel the room buzzing with frustration, and she couldn't blame them. "In the process I was caught by a janitor. He tried to detain me until the police arrived. I ran by him. He reached for me and slipped on the wet floor when I broke out of his grip."

"A little muddy on whether we can call that assault," Michael challenged, but he still looked unsatisfied that the whole story was out.

"What papers were you there to steal?" Piper asked, attempting to be some kind of lifeline for Shayna. "I'm sure if you felt you had to break into a place, there must have been a reason."

Michael held up a halting hand. "Can we not advocate for breaking and entering ever being excusable?"

Piper pushed his hand down and stared him square in the eye. "Can we not pretend there aren't ever reasons to break the law?"

Shayna reached down into her bag and pulled out a list. One she'd been reading over and over again for three weeks. "I needed a list of students from the Hillderstaff Indian Boarding School from 1957 to 1969."

"Why?" Piper pressed, imploring her to go on even though it was clear she was trying to hold back as much information as possible. "What did you need this list for?"

"There were two hundred fifty-seven names on the list," Shayna whispered. "Two hundred eleven are marked in red. They are deemed contained."

"Contained?" Michael asked, little flickers of anger morphing into worry. "What does that mean?"

"They have either died in recent years or have signed a legally binding nondisclosure agreement through mediation in return for money. There's a copy of an example of one on the back page," Shayna explained, handing the papers over to Michael. "They can't seek any legal recourse or speak publically about their time as students at the school."

Jules nibbled at her thumbnail as she looked from Shayna to Michael. "What would they need that for?"

Michael flipped through the papers and spoke up before Shayna could. "The boarding schools across the country had concerning practices. I'm sure it's related to that."

"What about the other forty-six students," Jules asked, a quiver in her voice. "The ones who hadn't been deemed, what did you call it?"

"Contained," Shayna repeated. "The remaining forty-six students have different notes on this list. There are forty-one marked with the letters DOD, and dates or at least months next to them. All between 1957 and 1969."

"Department of Defense?" Bobby asked, leaning over Michael's shoulder to look at the paper for himself.

"Date of death," Michael corrected grimly.

"Forty-one children died while students at the boarding school?" Betty cried out. "How can that be true?"

"As far as the world is concerned, it's not," Shayna said, the words feeling like sawdust in her mouth. "The story is one rabbit hole after another and too deep to go into tonight. Those forty-one kids can't be saved, but—"

"These five people," Michael said, his eyes getting wide with understanding, "haven't been 'contained,' and they aren't listed as dead."

"They can tell their story freely," Shayna explained, a small light flickering in her chest. She'd never call it hope. That was far too optimistic. "The Hillderstaff family has never been able to track these remaining people down. They may be able to answer what no one else has been able to. How did forty-one boys die during these years, where are they buried, and who is to blame?"

Michael read frantically over the back of the pages he'd been handed. "There is no document that can supersede someone's ability to report a murder. No statute of limitations or exchange of money can keep someone from reporting that."

"You know that, and I know that," Shayna agreed, "but the people who have signed these papers over the last thirty years only know what these people are capable of. They believe they will never be free of their threats and intimidation. The least they could do was get a little money to feed their families. They won't talk."

"But these five will?" Bobby asked, looking skeptical. "What makes you think any of them know anything at all?"

"I don't know," Shayna admitted. "But I know they've avoided the reach of these people for decades. There has to be a reason for that."

"What exactly do you want to accomplish from this?" Betty asked, a tenderness returning to her voice. "It's a lot to take on."

"My father," Shayna choked out. "I never really knew him. After Tao was born he died of liver failure. He drank himself to death. I spent most my life wondering why it had to be that way. Would he be proud of me? Were we too much for him?"

"His choices," Michael cut in. "That has everything to do with him and nothing to do with the kind of kid you are. Trust me."

"I know it has nothing to do with me," Shayna said, raising her chin confidently. "It has everything to do with them." She leaned in and pointed to a name on the list. "He knew what happened at the school because he was a student there."

"Shayna," Betty edged out carefully, "this is bigger than you can handle on your own. That seems very clear to me. I see it has a personal connection to your life, and sometimes that can cloud judgement."

"You asked me what I wanted to accomplish out of all of this," Shayna said, looking around at each of them. "I want to tell the real story of what happened at the Hillderstaff Indian Boarding School. I want the people who beat and tortured the children there to be brought to justice. I want the reign of the Hillderstaff family, still going on today, brought to an end. I want to tell my father's story, too. I always wanted to know why he was so broken. The answers are here."

The room was silent, only the humming of the fridge filled

Shayna's ears as she watched each person in the room try to process her words.

"I feel like now may be the right time to tell you," Nicholas said, nibbling anxiously at the inside of his cheek, "my name is Nicholas Evan Hillderstaff."

"I did not see that coming," Betty cried, clapping her hands together nervously. "Guess we'll be up a while. I don't know how you got into this. I don't know how you'll get out of it. But the least I can do is brew some damn strong coffee while we figure it out."

"I have a plan to get out of it," Shayna insisted, feeling like no one was listening. "This has been part of the plan actually. Although I didn't plan on getting tracked down tonight. I was going to make it look like I had left on a bus for the coast. But I was actually going to double back. Before I left I found one of these men on the list already. I've talked to him and recorded our conversation. He's willing to go on record. I think I can get to at least two more of these five people. If they validate what he's said, maybe someone will start to listen."

Michael's voice was softer but unwavering. "You have criminal charges pending against you. Essentially you're a fugitive. The longer this goes on, the more risk there is to you and your future. We can call in some favors and try to get you a fair hearing. There were complex factors we can introduce and some emotional stress as it relates to your father. We can get this settled for you."

"If you heard the tape," Shayna said coolly, "you'd understand why this isn't about just me getting out of trouble. This man's story would haunt you, the way it does me. But you can't get involved. I know you, all of you; once you start this you won't be able to stop. And it's not your war to fight."

"It's not much of a war if you're the only soldier," Jules said, leaning in and stroking Shayna's hair softly. "You know us. We can't walk away from you now. We won't."

"It's why I didn't want to tell you," Shayna admitted, a defeated sigh. "I was going to pass through town and leave enough evidence that I was heading to the coast."

"We all need to sleep on it," Michael said, wrapping an arm around Jules. "Don't brew that coffee tonight Betty. Save it for the morning."

Shayna nodded her head and yawned, the exhaustion of it all finally catching up with her.

"Gather up your kids from the yard," Betty ordered. "Shayna you can take the spare room upstairs. Your friend here can take the couch. The pillows and the blankets are free young man, as is the advice."

"Advice?" Nicholas asked quizzically, the corners of his mouth tentatively rising, but not making it into a full smile.

Betty leaned in close to Nicholas and explained. "I know every squeak in every floorboard from this couch to that bedroom upstairs. You, however, don't."

"I understand," Nicholas said, his cheeks blazing red. "I'm happy to stay on the couch."

"Then I'm happy not to hit you in the head with a cast iron skillet. Look at us, all happy. Hope we stay that way."

As if she hadn't just threatened a young man's life, Betty scurried out of the room humming. "Night to the rest of you. See you in the morning," she sang over her shoulder.

"She scares me a little," Nicholas whispered to no one in particular.

Michael shook his head as if he were disappointed. "If you're only a little scared, you're not paying enough attention."

CHAPTER 5

Shayna slept. Deep unimpeded slumber that she hadn't experienced in ages. It wasn't the quiet house or the extra fluffing Betty had done to the pillow. Her problems weren't solved. Her worry wasn't over. But when her eyes closed last night a sense of security overtook her, and she knew it was because of the people who'd now sworn to help her. If only they knew how fruitless their efforts would be.

"Morning," Shayna said, wiping the sleep from her eyes as she entered the kitchen. Nicholas was already up, digging into a proper stack of pancakes and nodding when Betty offered to refill his now empty glass of juice. "This is one of the best meals I've ever had, and I've eaten all over the world."

Betty's husband, Clay, was now in the kitchen too, unfolding his newspaper as he settled in the chair next to Nicholas. "I heard we had some excitement associated with this visit," he said, too cheery for the reality of it all, as if he were commenting on a new store opening in town.

"Sorry," Shayna groaned, nibbling at her lip as she made her way to Betty's side to carry the bacon to the table.

"No need to apologize," Clay corrected quickly. "We do just

fine around here with some excitement. Frankie is going to be coming in sometime this morning. I'm sure she'll be glad to help if she can."

"And Michael will have some answers, I'm sure of it," Betty asserted as she finally took a seat at the table. "There's always a way out of these kinds of things if we put our heads together."

"The tape," Nicholas said, his eyes darting away, knowing he was going to upset Shayna. "You think we could be of more help if we could hear it?"

"No," Shayna cut in. "It won't change anything. I gave him my word I wouldn't share the tape with anyone until the time was right."

"That's fine, dear," Betty said, patting her hand lightly, trying to calm her. "You made a promise and you stick by it. We can help you anyway."

"Hello," multiple voices called as they clamored in the screen door and spilled into the house.

"Everyone get a plate," Betty ordered as she popped out of her chair and started handing out hugs. "Kids, I set you up at the table in the other room. Go on in." Piper and Bobby's twins and Frankie's little brother scampered away. "Frankie, my girl, let me get a good squeeze on you."

"You're crushing me," Frankie protested, her words muffled by Betty's shoulder. "I need my ribs right where they are, please."

"Right where they are," Betty said, letting her go and poking at Frankie's side. "Where they are is sticking out. You are too thin, girl. Are you eating at college or what?"

"I'm fine, now let me see my friend, will you?" Frankie asked, playfully swatting her grandmother away and moving hastily to Shayna. "What the hell did you get yourself into?"

"It's bad," Shayna admitted, welcoming the hug and fighting the tears flooding her eyes. "It's really bad."

"Don't worry," Frankie said, gesturing for Shayna to sit back down and encouraging her to take a deep breath. "We'll handle it. You did the right thing by coming here."

Michael slid a couple pancakes onto his plate and sighed. "Coming was the right thing, but staying isn't. I had three phone calls from town already, saying Lyle was asking around about all of us and you. No one's giving you up as far as I can tell, but Edenville isn't big enough to hide out in until I can get some legal stuff sorted out for you. If you are adamant that you won't turn yourself in, then you need to make a plan."

"I'm going back," Shayna affirmed. "I have more people to interview. I know where one is, and I believe he'll talk to me. If he'll go on record, maybe there will be something that can't be ignored or covered up."

Jules folded her arms across her chest and shook her head. "It's dangerous. You're saying this Hillderstaff family is powerful and willing to do anything to silence this."

"If the people I'm interviewing aren't scared enough to stay silent," Shayna said confidently, "how can I use that as my excuse? They've endured things you can't imagine. They've seen things I wouldn't wish on my worst enemy. If they are willing to speak up, we should all be willing to listen."

"We are," Piper assured her. "You just don't have to be the only one to do it. We're a very capable group of adults."

"None of you are Native," Shayna explained. "They wouldn't trust you."

"So what do you propose?" Frankie asked, fixing her gaze on Shayna.

"Hang on," Michael interrupted, taking a big swig of his coffee. "Let's talk reality here for a moment. This would by no means be the first boarding school accused of abuse. There is precedence here, and I'll be honest, very little swings in our favor. Most statutes of limitations have run out. Even with a document that has dates and an abbreviation that might mean date of death, we have no evidence of murder. Could you tell the story of the school? Maybe. But with what actual evidence? If you're thinking you'll seek justice against actual individuals who participated in abuse, you, and the people you are talking to, should know it's not likely."

"The bodies," Shayna whispered. "That would be enough. We could prove something then."

Frankie wrinkled her brow thoughtfully as she considered the back and forth. "How could the families of the children not have reported them missing? You can't just kill dozens of children and expect no one comes looking for them."

"According to the first man I interviewed most of the children on this list were either orphans or abandoned by their families. The other children's parents went to HIBS looking for their kids," Shayna explained. "They begged and were all threatened and sent away. They were told their children ran away or were sent on work internships on the other side of the country. They were lied to and tricked. You aren't thinking about this through the lens of our people. Walking in to the police station and accusing the Hillderstaff family of murder would bring hellfire down on the parents."

Bobby seemed as though he couldn't stay quiet anymore. "If we're talking about murder, about a gravesite of some kind, then it ends here. I'll make a call to the FBI and get them involved. Michael's right, this isn't the first case of accusations of wide spread abuse and even unmarked graves associated with schools like this. They'll be better equipped to handle the situation."

Shayna felt her cheeks blazing red. "I need more time to be certain. If I leave now and get to these people quickly, I can get them to go on record. The first man I interviewed said two others on the list would know for sure where bodies were buried."

"And your father?" Betty asked, pursing her lips together. "Does he come up in these interviews?"

"Your father?" Frankie asked, clearly not aware of this important detail. "What does he have to do with this?"

"He was a student," Shayna admitted nervously. "There's something else I didn't mention last night. One of the five people on the list is my father's brother. My uncle Guyapi. I've never met him, but he may hold some answers if I can find him."

Frankie pressed, looking worried, "Your brother would want to know. He thinks your father's side of the family is dangerous and shifty. You might not like what you find."

"I don't have to like it," Shayna said, a bite in her voice. "And Tao doesn't need to be involved in this. He has enough on his plate, and I don't want them going after him, too."

Frankie stood up, her shoulders rigid with assertion. "I'll go with you. I have two weeks off for spring break. I was going to spend one week out there anyway. You can't do this by yourself."

"She's not exactly by herself." Nicholas, who seemed to be shell-shocked by this gaggle of voices and arguments, finally spoke up. "I'm going to be with her every step of the way."

"No offense there, Nicky," Betty said, waving her fork at him, "but we aren't sure whose side you're on in all of this. Your last name gives me pause as it relates to all of this."

"I understand," Nicholas nodded, but Shayna could tell he was annoyed. "I want the truth to come out as much as anyone else. Whoever was involved in the abuse at HIBS should be held responsible."

"And how about the rest of your family?" Betty challenged. "I can't imagine they'll want their name slandered and associated with these atrocities."

Nicholas shrugged. "I'm sure they won't. My father is a senator. My aunts and uncles are all CEOs of different branches of the family businesses. I haven't exactly lived up to their expectations over the years; I've always been somewhat on the outside."

Michael looked the most skeptical as he rubbed his tired eyes.

"And let's say this does come out. What do you think will happen to them? If it is what Shayna says, not only could their names be implicated, but if they contributed to any form of cover-up or conspiracy that occurred within the statute of limitations, they could be held criminally liable. Are you sure you'll know where your loyalties lie then?" The question was a sharp-edged sword, slicing to the heart of the matter.

"My loyalty is with the truth. It's with the people on that list. If all my name stands for is the atrocities of that school, then I don't want to be associated with it at all." Nicholas stood tall, though no one seemed to soften their expression.

The room was silent, an uncommon occurrence in Betty's kitchen. No one seemed ready to challenge Nicholas's loyalty any further, but no one seemed certain of it either. No more than they were certain what to do next.

Jules was the first to speak again. "I'm not comfortable with you three heading west alone. We're talking about some very serious things here."

"I can go with them," Piper offered, raising her hand, "if you can help Bobby with the twins while I'm there."

"Are you sure?" Jules asked, her face filling with worry. "I don't want you having to give up your vacation time to—"

"To follow my goddaughter and her best friend on one of those adventures you and I used to have?" Piper asked, lightening a little. "I was starting to get restless anyway with all the normalcy around here."

Michael let out a little huff. "You'd be the responsible adult in all of this. You do understand that, right? It's not some escapade to relive your youth."

Piper's brows raised nearly to her hairline, and her eyes grew wide. "I'm not sure what to be mad at, are you calling me irresponsible or old? I'm not reliving my youth. I'm still in it."

Jules gave him a whack across the arm and a stern look.

"There isn't anyone on earth I'd want out there with these kids besides the people in this room. Piper will keep them in line."

Bobby nodded his head in agreement. "I think it's a good idea. The twins and I will be fine, and I know Piper can keep things under control there."

Betty hummed as she looked at them all, like a judge getting ready to rule on a difficult case. Shayna watched as her eyes fell on Nicholas, lingering an extra beat. "If things get out of hand, I want to know about it right away. This has the potential to get stickier than molasses on asphalt in August."

Michael sighed and ran his hand through his salt and peppered hair. "You'll have to drive if you don't want to raise any flags with the police. I can't believe I'm advising you to avoid the police, but I'm going to be looking deeper into the charges against you. Stay off the radar until I can come up with something. Make your case, get your interviews, but there's a time limit on how long I'll be supportive of this."

Piper started ticking things off on her fingers. "So evade the police, inject ourselves into a deep conspiracy, and try to unearth a long buried story. Got it."

Jules wrapped an arm around her worried-looking husband and rested her head on his shoulder. "You're going to make his head explode."

"They are going to make me change my mind," Michael corrected, grinding his teeth. "Just do me one favor," Jules said seriously, some of the optimism in her voice started melting away. "It's hot as the surface of the sun out there. Pack extra sunscreen."

Piper let out a breathy laugh. "Yes, Mom."

CHAPTER 6

Shayna had given up on getting the aching knot out of her shoulder. It would just be a permanent throbbing pain now. Four days in the car, all driving in shifts, there was no way to stay comfortable. "You want to switch?" she asked Piper, whose eyes were fixed on the dark road ahead of her. "I've been driving on these desert roads for years."

"I can't get over how dark it is," Piper said, squinting. "But the sun should be coming up soon. We can switch then."

"Actually," Shayna said, turning around to peek at Frankie and Nicholas sleeping in the backseat. "I think we should go straight to the contact I have. I don't want to lose any more time."

"I know what that feels like," Piper said earnestly. "I've been in your shoes, and the urgency can bring you down in the end. We've been driving for days, are you sure you're in the right state of mind to do this?"

"Hakan Greywolf has been hiding for forty years," Shayna said, trying to sit up straighter and look wide awake. "I have a map to find him, and I don't think he'll turn me away. Once he knows others are coming forward, I'm sure he'll want to as well."

"I think we should drop them off," Piper suggested, nodding at the backseat. "I think the less people the better."

"You don't trust Nicholas," Shayna whispered, watching to see if he stirred from his sleep. "I could see the way you were all looking at him. It was obvious."

"Good," Piper said. "I don't think any of us were trying to be inconspicuous. You have to admit with something so sensitive it's dangerous to involve someone in the family you are trying to expose."

"I trust him," Shayna replied, tipping her chin up. "There are things you don't know. He's more than proved his loyalty to me."

"It's a moving target," Piper said with a sigh. "People's loyalties are not finite. They change. Circumstances change. I'm just saying I think we should drop them off at your house first."

"We'll have to double back this way almost two hours," Shayna protested. "Are you sure you can deal with that much more time in the car?"

"You'd be amazed what I can deal with when I want to get something done," Piper assured her. "Like I said, I know what you're feeling right now, that burning need to do something, anything that makes a difference. You want to right all the wrongs, but you should know no matter what you do, it won't feel the way you think it will."

"What do you mean?" Shayna asked, a shot of pain in her chest at the thought that she might fail. And that Piper believed she would. "I'm going to do this."

"I'm not saying you won't, I'm saying it never feels as good as you think it will. The more stories you hear, the more people you interview, it does something to you. I'm a social worker. My day is filled with stories, and for every inch of progress I make, there's a mile more to go. There was a time I was trying to fill my holes by bringing justice to others. It only makes more holes."

"Then why do you do it?" Shayna snapped, her nerves raw

from the endless road trip. "If it's so terrible why not do something else?"

"The only thing worse than doing it," Piper admitted, "is doing nothing at all. I'm not trying to convince you to stop. I'm not saying you'll fail. I'm warning you that at the end of all of this, no matter how it turns out, you'll be different. And it won't necessarily be for the better."

Shayna shook her head and pressed her lips together tightly. A few things came to mind that she might say, but in her heart she believed Piper was probably right. From everything she knew about Piper's past, she was an expert on pain and disappointment.

"Let's drop them off," Shayna said, as she pressed her head against the glass of the passenger window and stared into the darkness. This stretch of road was like all the others she'd traveled on, her mother in the driver's seat and her the lookout. You never knew what a night this dark could bring.

"Stop," Shayna shrieked suddenly, and Piper slammed on the brakes, sending the car into a fishtail skid.

There in front of the bright headlights was a mangy looking coyote staring straight at them. Everyone in the car was now awake, and all of them except Shayna were gasping and holding their chests.

Unrolling her window she called out. "Move on," she ordered, staring the mutt in the eyes. "Back into the night." A second later his eyes darted away, and as fast as he'd appeared he was gone.

"That was close," Frankie said, leaning over the front seat. "You stopped just in time."

Piper took her foot off the brake and eased the car forward. "It came out of nowhere. How did you even see it coming, Shayna?"

"My brother would say I could sense him," Shayna explained wearily. "He would call it an omen and remind me that anything can come from the darkness to block your path. Only vigilance can protect you."

"You don't agree?" Frankie asked, now resting her chin on the back of Shayna's seat.

"It's a wild animal running in the dark. It's no sign from the spirits," Shayna countered. "They don't have signs for people like me who have strayed from them. I'm a fallen follower. No one watches over me."

"I don't know," Piper said, picking up speed and confidence now that the scare was over. "You've got Betty on your side. That's always been enough protection for me. I think it'll do for now."

CHAPTER 7

"A little warning would have been nice," Tao grumbled at his sister and looked over at the train of people coming in behind her. "Are you having a party?" His eyes widened at the sight of Frankie, and Shayna had to stifle a laugh.

"I brought your girlfriend; be happy about that." The look on his face shifted from excitement to awkward frustration.

"You should have called," he said gruffly as he pulled a shirt over his head.

"The phone's been cut off," Shayna reminded him. "I'm surprised the power is still on."

"Hello Tao," Piper announced, tossing her bag off her shoulder and onto the floor. "I'm sorry we're just popping in like this. It's a long story. But we're looking for a home base."

"Does this have anything to do with the cops looking for you?" Tao asked, nodding his chin at Frankie coolly and then eyeing Nicholas with some reservation. "They sent a message through a few people off the reservation saying they were looking for you. Assault?"

"Like Piper said, it's a long story, and I'm not getting into it right now. Piper and I have someplace to be. This is Nicholas.

He's my friend. Play nice." Shayna pointed a threatening finger at her brother and cocked a challenging brow in his direction.

"You really think you can just blow in here and not explain what's going on?" Tao laughed humorlessly, puffing out his chest. "If you don't tell me, Frankie will."

"Ah, I knew this day would come," Shayna said, folding her arms over her chest and grimacing at them both. "Time to pick your loyalties, Frankie. Is it me, your longtime devoted friend who loves you, or the guy you are sort of dating."

"I pick him," Frankie said quickly. "Not out of loyalty but because he should know what's going on. You know he can help."

"I know he can try to tell me what I'm doing is crazy." Shayna had one handle on the doorknob and was eyeing Piper, trying to indicate they should leave.

Tao sat down on the chair in the corner. "You found out Dad went to HIBS, and now you're on some crusade to expose what went on there." A look of victory spread across his face.

"How do you know that?" Shayna asked, throwing daggers with her eyes at everyone in the room as though they'd betrayed her.

"Relax," he said coolly. "No one here gave you up. I got as much info as I could about the charges against you, and I put it together from there. I already knew Dad went to school there. The place you broke into, who it was owned by, I figured it out. So what, you're trying to get Dad some justice or something? Trust me, it's not worth it. Nothing is going to redeem that man's legacy."

"I have a list," Shayna said, drawing in a deep breath. "This has nothing to do with Dad. There are people I think will go on record and speak publicly against the Hillderstaff family and the people who worked at the school."

"Why?" Tao asked, twisting his face skeptically. "A law suit? You think you can get them reparation? I'm sure most of the people on your list are living a life where extra money won't make a difference. They have way bigger problems than bills."

"No. I'm doing it because the Hillderstaff family is walking around as if nothing ever happened. Look at us," she said, gesturing around at the house. "They ruined generations of this family. If Dad hadn't gone to that school, he'd probably still be alive. Maybe he wouldn't have drunk himself to death."

"Maybe Mom wouldn't have cancer," Tao offered, though it wasn't layered with condescension but an attempt to remind her of reality. "Life isn't going to be easy for us, Shayna, even if you do this, whatever it is you think you're doing. Everyone knows the Hillderstaff family is a bunch of arrogant, money-grabbing monsters who don't do a damn thing for anyone but themselves."

"This feels like a good time to let you know my full name," Nicholas said, wiping his sweaty hand on his shorts and extending it to Tao. "I'm Nicholas Hillderstaff. I figure while we're getting everything out, I may as well tell you now."

Tao didn't accept the handshake or let his face even flinch with shock. He stared straight at Nicholas and let the awkward-ness fill the room like a bubble. Something a proper guy like Nicholas with all his years of etiquette training could not let linger.

"I know what you're thinking now—" Nicholas started, but Tao cut him off, jumping to his feet and extending to his full height. He stood only an inch or two taller, but the move had Nicholas stumbling backward.

"I highly doubt you know what I'm thinking, considering we have absolutely nothing in common. There is nothing in my life you can relate to. But tell me why you are here and make it a damn good reason."

"I care about your sister," Nicholas said, standing up straight again. "I want to help."

"Great," Tao said, a wide smile spreading across his face.

Shayna knew it was a trap. "Give your grandfather a call, and let him know he should come clean about everything that happened at the school. Have him go on record and admit he was running a house of torture. That's how you can help my sister right now."

"I don't know who is behind what happened at the school. He owned it," Nicholas corrected evenly, "but he didn't run it. It's not like he was in there every day doing something wrong. So even if I went to him—"

Shayna bit into his words like a cobra striking from across the room. "Nicholas, you can't honestly believe your grandfather didn't at least know and condone what was happening there. It's more likely the employees of the school were following his orders."

"He isn't that kind of man," Nicholas defended. "He's from a different generation, and I don't agree with everything he says, but he wouldn't order children to be treated that way. He wouldn't."

Shayna felt the arrows that had been pointed at her heart for weeks pierce her. He'd been saying all the right things. *Justice had to be found no matter the expense. No matter who suffered in the process. Anyone responsible had to pay.* The one piece that hadn't slid into place until right then was that Nicholas didn't believe his grandfather would ever be held accountable, because he thought he couldn't be guilty. Maybe Nicholas could admit his family took part in some complicit way that society could forgive. But in his eyes, the man he knew never held the leather strap and struck a child. He never withheld food for days. He never even knew it was happening. The problem was, Shayna knew different.

"Piper." Shayna sighed, realizing something dramatic had just shifted between them. "I think we should go. I want to get these people on record as soon as possible."

"Where is your mother?" Piper asked, turning her gaze toward

Tao. They were all technically adults, but Piper clearly recognized the tension building, and some supervision wouldn't hurt.

Tao scratched at his head nervously, the way he always did when he worried. "She's staying with her sister. Something happened with the clinical trial she was part of, so they are trying to figure out what to do next. She's getting some treatment at the clinic on reservation."

"It was them," Shayna announced, forcing herself not to look at Nicholas. "The Hillderstaff family have ties to that hospital; they are trying to send me a message."

"Shayna," Tao's voice boomed, "that was her best chance at beating this. How can you—? We have to . . ." he stuttered, the shockwaves overtaking him as he paced the room.

"I'm going to fix this," Shayna promised. "I'm going to show everyone the truth, and when I expose them they'll have no choice but to put Mom back in the clinical trial."

The room fell silent as Tao seemed to process how deep this hole was and how hard it would be to climb out. "Faster," Tao said flatly. "We do this faster then. You get as many people willing to talk on the record as possible. I'll talk to people on the reservation to make sure you're protected while you're here. That cop looking for you won't get a foot on this land without me getting a heads-up. What else?"

Nicholas fidgeted uncomfortably in the corner of the room. "I know where I think there might be more records about the years you are looking for at the school. I can get you in the building. I can get access."

Tao grunted his reply. "When it incriminates them, will you still turn over what you find?"

"I'll get you in," Nicholas replied. "Where it goes from there is up to you. I want the truth too."

"No one does anything until we get back," Piper insisted, pointing her finger at everyone. "I can't believe I'm saying this, but, Frankie, you're in charge. Keep these guys from killing each other before morning. Gets some food, get some sleep, and keep your phone on."

"Where is it?" Tao asked Shayna, rushing his words to catch her before they could leave. "Where are you going?"

"It's behind the Three Spoke Mountain. I'm looking for a man named Hakan Greywolf."

"I know his family," Tao said, hurrying toward the door as if he might get an invite. "I went to school with his grandson. I don't think he's a very welcoming guy. Especially if he's up on those mountains. You don't live up there if you want company."

Shayna opened the front door, stepped quickly through it, and didn't look back. "I've got this, Tao."

CHAPTER 8

"This can't be right," Piper whispered, afraid to disrupt the eerie silence of the mountainside. "The road ended back there. This is barely a path. The guy we're going to meet is in his seventies; he can't possibly live up here."

"These are the directions Aponi gave me. He was certain this is where the house is. Just up around this bend. Watch your step. This cactus will take you down in a hurry if you bump it." Shayna hadn't been walking in the mountains for a long time. It had been all campus commons and dorm room halls. Even before she'd started college she'd stopped thinking of nature as an escape the way she had as a very young child. When things became difficult you walked, weaving through brush and baking under the heat of the summer sun until the world faded away. But recently, coming into the mountains was a source of guilt. Something Tao reminded her she'd abandoned.

As the rocks slid beneath Shayna's feet, she remembered how she'd learned to anticipate their movements and shift her weight. No step was taken for granted. No movement was done without forethought.

Piper stumbled and searched for a steady path that didn't seem to exist, and Shayna felt a twinge of pride. "Step here," she said, and pointed behind her. "Move your foot like this, between this low brush."

"It's hot," Piper moaned, twisting her hair into a ponytail and panting animatedly. "I've never been to the desert before."

"Really?" Shayna asked, astonished. "I always think of you as worldly. I figured you've been just about everywhere."

"Not even close," Piper laughed, patting at her glistening forehead. "There were no vacations for me when I was a kid. It was just survival. Then when I was older there were other things that kept me from seeing the world. There isn't much I would change though."

"Frankie told me about some of the stuff you had going on," Shayna said sheepishly, unsure if Piper was opening a door for her to walk through or not.

Piper laughed sarcastically. "Frankie doesn't know half of the skeletons in my closet. She's heard bits and pieces I'm sure, but most she wouldn't believe if I told her."

"Well, um," Shayna stuttered, "we kind of researched it one summer. We treated it like a school project. It sounds stupid when I say it now. You know how we always pretended we were private investigators? We were curious kids. So we found out about The Railway Killer and stuff that happened to you."

"Yeah," Piper said, her voice dropping some but not filling with anything Shayna would consider anger. "I figured her curiosity would win out one day, and she'd try to look into my past. But what you'll find are the stories printed in the paper, and the ones you see floating out in the world don't tell you the whole truth. It's not until you know how someone felt, what they feared, who they trusted, and what they lost. That's when you know the real story. People look at my connection to Bobby, Michael, Jules, and Betty, and they find it strange. I know that. Here I am, some girl from up north with no ties to anyone, and then suddenly I'm connected to these people in a way most could never comprehend. We experienced things that connected us in a way that can never be broken."

"Like what?" Shayna asked, speaking thoughtfully as she was walking. Every word had to be carefully crafted.

"Well," Piper said, looking up at the sky and contemplating the question, "I grew up with a monster, but I thought I was the only one left he would hurt. Turns out he was a serial killer. I guess you knew that part."

"Sort of," Shayna shrugged. "But he came after you in Edenville?"

"He did. I was unfinished business for him. It haunted him that I had survived his attack. No one else had. My mother hadn't."

"He killed her, right?" Shayna asked, swallowing hard. "That must have been so awful."

"It was," Piper admitted. "You think the only thing someone might feel in that situation is sadness, but it's important for you to understand a survivor has many complicated emotions. Guilt. I carried so much guilt with me. Whatever you think these people are feeling when you talk to them, know that it's probably more complex than you assume."

"Sorry," Shayna apologized instinctively, "I hope that didn't come across as rude. I'm always fascinated by how you've redesigned your life."

"Don't be sorry," Piper said, waving her off. "I'm not trying to scare you either. No matter what they've experienced, their life is theirs to live. It took time for me to realize there is another side to pain. It's a coin. It flips on you all the time, but you're never stuck on one side for too long."

"There," Shayna said, pointing to a small stone structure half tucked into a boulder formation. "I'm not trying to be rude. I hope you know it's a cultural thing, but you shouldn't do much talking."

"Fair enough," Piper said, her hand gripping the cramp in her side. "Shouldn't be a problem since I can't even catch my breath. Guess I better get back to the gym when I get home."

Shayna walked to the door cautiously, knowing it was rarely knocked on unexpectedly. "Greywolf," she called as she tapped on the wood door.

Piper took refuge from the sun under the shade cast by the boulders. "These rocks aren't going to just topple over, are they?" she asked, looking precariously at the jagged pile of car-sized boulders.

"They haven't for all these years," Shayna assured her as footsteps in the house began growing louder. "Greywolf," Shayna announced again as she fished the photograph out of her pocket.

"Are you the spirit of the wind or are you real?" a kind faced man asked as he opened the wood door and squinted his coal black eyes at them. The smell of a familiar earthy musk poured out with him. He would be just a handful of years older than her father would have been. Maybe they would look similar. Maybe they'd smell the same.

"We are real, Greywolf," Shayna said, holding the photograph out for him to see. "This is my father. Did you know him?"

"I did," Greywolf said, averting his eyes away from the photograph as though he already knew what she would ask him next.

"You knew him from school?" she asked. "He would have been a young boy as you left HIBS.

"Yes," Greywolf said. "Did they kill him too?"

"No," Shayna bit back quickly. "Not directly, but he is dead now. His liver."

"How did you know I was here?" Greywolf asked, looking past them to the edge of the mountain as if they may have brought the rest of the world with them, opening a portal for anyone to waltz through.

"Aponi drew a map. I talked with him, and he told me to seek you out," Shayna said, choosing her worlds carefully. "He told me to speak to the spirit within you."

"You want to know about the school? About the people there?" Greywolf asked, still standing in his doorway and not welcoming them in. "I won't speak with her," he said, jutting his chin over to Piper. "She is an outsider."

"I understand," Piper said, tossing her hands up disarmingly. "I am happy to stay out of the way, but you should know I am such an outsider, not from here, that I will fry like an egg if you make me stay outside. I'm not built for the heat."

Greywolf's leathery face rose and fell with a chuckle he couldn't hold back. "There is a sitting room here," he offered, gesturing just inside the door. "It's cool. You can help yourself to a drink in the fridge."

"Thank you," Piper said, clasping her hands together in gratitude and huffing as though she'd been holding her breath. "I don't know how you get used to this heat."

"You don't get used to it," Greywolf corrected. "You outsmart it. You trick it. Who are you anyway?"

"She is like my akacita. My peacekeeper. My brother did not want me to come up here alone. My friends did not want me doing this without help. She's keeping the peace, so I can be here." Shayna hoped her explanation would satisfy him, but skeptics were usually proven right in their community.

"Why didn't your brother come with you himself then?" Greywolf asked suspiciously.

"Because he bothers me," Shayna admitted with a smile. "He thinks he knows better than I do. We don't agree on many things, and I don't want to deal with that."

"Yes," Greywolf chuckled again. "Your truth speaks to me.

Come to the yard." Shayna waved a quick reassurance to Piper before she and Greywolf navigated the maze of belongings piled up in the dim but cool house that was mostly cement and stone. When they reached the back of the house, Greywolf slid the wood door aside and gestured to some rocks in the shade. "Why do you want to know these things?" he asked her, groaning as he lowered himself onto a cool rock across from where she sat.

"People should know the truth," Shayna said quietly, trying to show this elder an abundance of respect. "People should know what happened."

"No," he said, shaking his head and shaggy gray and black hair back and forth. "That isn't a reason to be here. It isn't your reason. Tell me *your* truth."

"Uh," Shayna said, fumbling over her words, "I think the Hillderstaff family should be held accountable for what they did, what they allowed to happen to our people. To you." She couldn't level her gaze at him as she continued to lie.

"You don't know me," Greywolf challenged, placing his dark spotted hand on his chest. "Your pity is not enough to compel you all this way. I'm sure it has not been easy."

"It hasn't," she huffed, each failure and set back over the last few weeks hitting her like a hot poker pulled from the fire.

"The day is long," Greywolf said, gazing up at the cloudless blue sky that was only broken by mountain peaks in the distance. "My days here are not. The medicine man says I am not long for this earth."

"I'm sorry," Shayna said, life's unforgiving reality clenching tighter on her heart. "I didn't know you were sick."

"I am one of the lucky ones, wouldn't you say?" he asked, turning his deep-set, haunting eyes toward her.

"Lucky for being sick?"

"Lucky to have lived this long. So many I have grown up with have taken their own lives. Or died with a bottle to their lips. I don't drink."

"That's good," Shayna said, offering a small smile. "I've seen so many lives ruined by it."

"No," Greywolf corrected, waving his finger at her. "The alcohol is a medicine. The mind is sick, and they only try to treat it. I haven't found a way to blame them for trying to make themselves hurt less."

"There are other ways," Shayna said, a scolding tone to her voice as she imagined her father and all he could have been had he lived.

"Tell me your truth," Greywolf insisted again. "Why do you want to know? Remember my days are short. I don't wish to spend much more of it in this way with you."

Shayna drew in a deep breath and let the words she'd been stuffing down fizz to the surface like bubbles from the bottom of the sea. "I want to know what my father lived through, so I can know why he had to drink until he died. Why was he so broken? Then I want the Hillderstaff family to suffer for that. Not only for what they did back then but for what they are still doing."

Greywolf nodded his head and closed his eyes, silently letting her know she'd rung the right bell. "Now?" he asked, after the few long beats of silence. "What are they doing now?"

"Trying to silence me," Shayna explained, trying to capitalize on the impact this was having on Greywolf. The look on his face told her that these people still causing pain did not sit well with him. "They have taken away medicine my mother needs. They had me kicked out of school. I've stolen something from them, and they want it back, along with my agreement to leave this alone."

"What have you stolen?" Greywolf asked, the mischievous sparkle in his eye beginning to dance.

"A list," Shayna said, pulling the papers from her bag. "These are all the students that attended HIBS before it closed. All these are people who took money in exchange for their silence or their safety. But these, you being one of them, can speak as freely as you like about what happened there."

"Your uncle Guyapi," Greywolf noted. He scanned and then pointed to his name and then another. "Aponi."

"And you know the others?" Shayna asked, full of hope. Aponi had only known the whereabouts of Greywolf. She needed a few reliable people willing to go on record, and she hoped Greywolf could lead her to more. With the jagged nail of his pointer finger he made slashes through the two remaining names who were not her uncle.

"Dead," he explained somberly. It is just Aponi, your uncle, and me. We are the only ones left who would not take their money or bend to their threats."

"So you knew they were looking for you? You knew what they wanted?"

"Yes," Greywolf said firmly. "They called me Thomas Merry. All the students were given new white names. Most kept them. I did not. And when they came to look for us, we gave no trail under the names and lives they tried to force on us. We moved many times and lived a life they couldn't understand enough to find us."

"To what end?" Shayna asked, dying to reach into her bag and get her tape recorder. Something told her it was too soon to try.

Greywolf chuckled. "So we would have peace. So they could not do to us what they have done to you and your family."

"Didn't you ever want to stop them?" Shayna asked, watching how her words worked like a brush to paint a new, far sadder expression on his face.

"There is a cavernous difference between our generations. Yours and mine. You were told you could do anything. You were made to believe one person had the power to stop people like them."

"I know I can," Shayna lied, desperate to convince him this cause was worth the risk to him.

"Your spirit," Greywolf replied on the tail end of a long breath. "It is much like your father's. He was a hard child to forget. Always getting himself into trouble. Running away. Bucking like a bronco against the saddle."

"I wouldn't know if we're alike. I never had the opportunity to find out."

"They took many men from their families. In one way or another they destroyed them."

"And they should pay for that. The world should know."

Greywolf seemed to be giving his responses great thought. "We were all like eggs when we arrived at the school. Full of life. Of potential for what we might turn into. But the longer you stayed, the more cracks formed. Many smashed to pieces."

"Can I put on my tape recorder now?" Shayna asked meekly. "Aponi spoke very freely and directly about his experiences, but I would like to have multiple statements to confirm what he said. Would you be willing to be one of them?"

Greywolf closed his eyes again as if the answer was being whispered in his ear. "The truth of Aponi is my truth too. Does it do you good to hear it twice?"

"It will help make the story believable," Shayna explained.

"Do you not believe?" Greywolf asked, tilting his head to the side and gazing at her with worry in his eyes.

"I do," Shayna called back quickly. "Sitting with Aponi, listening to him talk, it changed me. It pained me. But others, people who do not understand our people, they will want to know that you all speak the same truth."

"You may record me," Greywolf said, waving a hand at her

backpack and granting her permission. "But I will not answer all your questions."

"I understand," Shayna said, excitedly pulling her phone from her bag and queuing up the recording option. She spoke clearly as she turned it on. "I'm sitting here with Thomas Greywolf, a student of Hillderstaff Indian Boarding School. He is here of his own volition and speaking under no duress or coercion. Greywolf, can you tell me what your time at HIBS was like?"

"No," Greywolf answered flatly, and Shayna's heart jumped nervously in her chest. "I can show you," he announced, creaking slowly to his feet. He turned his back to her and with great effort pulled the back of his shirt up, exposing thick scars. Lash marks.

"Uh, Greywolf has just shown me his back, which appears to be covered with scars. Were these inflicted at HIBS?" Shayna asked and used her phone to snap some pictures. Greywolf turned back around and sat down again.

"Yes," Greywolf said, his voice loud and projecting. "A leather belt, with a metal handle was always used."

"As punishment?" Shayna asked, trying to force herself to not lead him in any one direction.

"I guess in their eyes." Greywolf shrugged. "What were we punished for? Speaking our language. Wishing to grow our hair back after they'd shaved it. Sneaking food when we were on rations penalty."

"Rations penalty?" Shayna asked, already knowing the meaning of the phrase as it was explained by Aponi, but needing to record it again.

"If we were not doing what they wanted, they would take away our food. We'd be starved until we would do as they asked. I made it six days once."

"Six days without food? What were they trying to get you to do that you wouldn't?" Shayna held her breath, wondering how closely his story would match her last interview.

"I had a leather pouch filled with things from home," Greywolf explained, using his hands to show the size of the old treasure. "Another student, trying to win favor with the supervisors, told them I had been hiding this pouch. They wanted to know where it was, but I never told them."

"Why did you have to hide it?" Shayna asked, the sweat gathering on her palms. "They were your belongings, right?"

"We weren't allowed anything from the reservation. The school, they wanted us to forget our heritage, our language, and our ways. I'd taken a small stone statue my grandfather had carved, a woven piece of cloth from my mother, and two drawings from my aunt. It wasn't as if I kept them with me. I couldn't risk that. Instead I kept them buried out in the sand a few hundred yards beyond the school's property."

"When it was found you were punished?" Shayna asked, averting her gaze as though that lent him some kind of privacy.

"I was put on rations and taken to the shack," Greywolf stated.

"What is the shack?" Shayna pressed, remembering the cold chill that ran up her spine when she'd heard Aponi describe it for the first time.

"It sat by the property, tucked under some boulders. There was nothing in it but a mattress on the floor and a hook on the wall."

"What was kept on the hook?" Shayna pressed, licking at her dry lips.

"The Lash," Greywolf said, holding his voice steady. "It was what they used to whip us. We'd be brought to the shack in groups of three. They never wanted us to get beaten without a witness."

"Why would they want that?"

"It didn't do them any good to beat us in private where none of the other kids could see how bad it was. They knew fear was more powerful than any desert wind."

"Who?" Shayna asked, her voice falling to a whisper, dictated by the moment and not by her vocal cords anymore.

"I only know them by the names they told us. Oxford. He was a tall skinny man with hair the color of Sedona clay. He was more freckles than not. The gap in his teeth was wide enough to stick a grape in, I bet. And he was mean. Angry all the time."

"And he beat you with the lash?" Shayna asked, knowing Aponi had already confirmed this man to be one of the worst at the school.

"Yes. And his fists. His boots. A rock once when I ran out of the shack before he was done with the lash. I was brought into the nurse's station that day, and they demanded I be taken to the hospital for my injuries. I was bleeding badly from a cut on my head, and my eyes were nearly swollen shut. My clothes had to be peeled away because of the blood on my back. But Oxford refused and told them they could clean me up or leave me on the floor, he didn't care. But I was not to be taken to the hospital."

Shayna drew in a deep breath and considered what she should ask next. The details mattered, and as she formulated her next question a tiny beeping filled the space between them.

"My watch," Greywolf explained, staring down at the banged up plastic timepiece on his wrist. "It's time for me to take my medicine."

"We can take a break," she said, fumbling to turn off the recorder. "Can I talk to my friend?"

"Help yourself to a drink," he said, the smile and warmth drained from his face. "I'll be upstairs for a little while. I have to lie down after I take my medicine. You'll still be here when I come down?"

"If that's what you want," Shayna replied timidly as she followed him into the house. She needed much more than he had given so far and leaving now might mean the end of their conversation.

"Fix yourself anything in the kitchen. I hardly eat these days. Most of the food my niece brings me up here goes to waste."

"Thank you," Shayna said, their eyes meeting for a moment, and she knew he understood the gratitude went deeper than the snacks he was offering.

As she walked into the small kitchen Piper popped to her feet and looked concerned. "Everything go all right?"

"He needs a break," Shayna said, swallowing hard. "I could use one too."

"How bad is it, Shayna?" Piper asked, eyeing her closely and waiting for some kind of indication.

"They were the worst kind of monsters," Shayna said, leaning against the cool stone wall. "The kind no one was trying to stop."

CHAPTER 9

Greywolf had settled into a chair in his living room and seemed to change his mind about Piper's presence. Maybe it was the way she'd stayed completely silent and pretended to busy herself, looking at some simple art on the wall. Or maybe it was his sheer and obvious exhaustion that opened him up in front of this stranger.

"Turn that thing back on," he said, gesturing at Shayna's phone. "You can record again. You asked about Oxford. You wanted to know who he was."

"Aponi didn't know his full name," Shayna said, switching her recorder back on. "Do you know who he is?"

"Yes," Greywolf said. "I saw him ten years after I left the school. I had taken a job on a railway doing some repairs, and he was a passenger. The job kept me far enough away from home where I felt they couldn't find me easily. I was hitching a ride back to the reservation on the evening train, and there he was. I don't know that he recognized me, but I knew him right away." Greywolf rose and shuffled to a drawer in a desk by the window. "I stole his ticket stub when he got up to go to the bathroom. I guess we've both stolen from them."

"You kept it?" Shayna asked in amazement as he handed it over. "Linden B. Oxford," she read as she squinted at the now faded ticket. "That's incredible."

"Hardly any of them went by their full names. When I got older I realized it was shame that kept them from giving their names. When the Hillderstaff family came by, even they would try to hide themselves in some way."

"Who from the Hillderstaff family would come?" Shayna asked, trying to steady her voice.

"The old man. Gregory Hillderstaff would come once a month. Most people wouldn't know that, but I worked in the laundry room, and he'd always park his big fancy car right behind our building. He'd meet with the supervisors out back. Give them orders and most times he'd leave right from there. Some days he'd bring his brothers. Those were the bad visits."

"How were they bad?" Shayna asked, her heart thumping so loud she thought it might echo off the stone walls. From what she'd learned so far the Hillderstaff brothers, who would be Nicholas's great uncles, were the cruelest arm of the organization.

"When the brothers came, and I don't know their names, they'd tell Oxford and the other supervisors they weren't doing a good enough job. The brothers' eyes would flame with anger, and they'd demand more."

"More what?" Shayna asked when Greywolf hesitated.

Drooping his shoulders, Greywolf closed his eyes to reply. "More blood spilled from the savage children. More Indians who had been changed. Converted. Assimilated. Broken from their ways and torn from their families in a more permanent way."

"Why would they want to do that?" Shayna asked, fully educated on the colonialism and genocide of her culture, but knowing for this recording it had to be broken down and spoken.

"That was why we were there. To be changed. We couldn't speak our language. Celebrate our customs. They wanted us to pray to their God. Live by their rules. No part of us was to remain besides our bodies. And even our bodies could only exist in the form they allowed. If they could have bleached our skin and molded our features to be like theirs, I believe they would have. Our minds were to be completely transformed."

"Did they all use those words?" Shayna asked. "Or was that understood, an unwritten rule."

"Ha," Greywolf chuckled at her question. "These were the words written on the large plaque outside the dining hall." He put his finger in the air as though he were reading along with them, the plaque clear in his mind's eye.

In mercy, rather than exterminate the masses of savagery, we will bestow on them the civility and knowledge of our culture, no matter the difficulties it imparts on us. We will persevere."

Greywolf whispered the last line again. "We will persevere. And they did. They left an undeniable effect on generations. The school was around from the turn of the century, opened by Gregory Hillderstaff Sr. If you can believe it, he was no more than your age and told people this was his life's passion."

"I can't imagine that being anyone's passion," Shayna cut back. "But I do know this happened all over the country, starting in the eighteen hundreds, but the legacy of the Hillderstaff School lived on well after the Meriam Report."

"What's that?" Piper interjected, looking instantly regretful that she had. "Sorry. I didn't mean to interrupt."

"It's all right." Greywolf sighed. "The things people don't know about this could fill a canyon. For all the information that's now at your fingertips, somehow this is still a secret."

Shayna, pleased to have gotten permission, began to explain the history of Indian boarding schools. It would give context to the recorded interview. "The Meriam Report came out in 1928 by the Brookings Institute. It was meant to give an overall assessment of indigenous people and the conditions they were living in.

It was about forty or more years after the first boarding schools were opened."

"Why were they started at all," Piper asked, emboldened to now engage in the conversation.

"It was the churches," Greywolf explained. "They set up schools on the reservations. They were paid by the government to educate the native children in hopes they could civilize them. The schools popped up everywhere. They were kidnapping children, beating them into submission, and forcing assimilation. When the Meriam Report came out, I'm told many thought we would find relief."

"Not so," Shayna said solemnly. "The report made endless recommendations about the changes that should be made. The education of indigenous people suffered under the then-current standards. They thought education should be moved back to the communities, the reservations. In spite of this, the Indian boarding schools continued to thrive. Some churches still went to reservations and, with the support of local law enforcement, essentially kidnapped children. Other students were orphans, their parents having died young from leftover trauma from their time in the boarding schools. Attendance grew. Abuse continued. Nothing changed. No one spoke up."

Greywolf attempted to stand again and then thought better of it when what seemed like a dizzy spell overtook him. "Would you get me that pot?" he asked Piper, who jumped up obediently. "There is something else I want to show you."

She hurried the softball-sized clay pot over to him, and he looked inside with a smile. "They never found the things I had buried," he said proudly, pulling out the items he'd brought with him to HIBS and had hidden from the staff. "When I was low, I would sneak away and remember what I had been taught before I went to that school."

"You said the Hillderstaff brothers were the worst. Their

names were Carlton and Gleason. Here is a picture of them," Shayna said, pulling out another photograph that had been cut from a newspaper. "Carlton on the left, Gleason on the right."

Greywolf switched abruptly to his native tongue and spoke so quickly and quietly Shayna could not make out his words. His wrinkled bent fingers pushed the paper away.

"I never knew their names," Greywolf said, his hand now crumpled into a shaking fist. "They were monsters in fine suits. No matter how bad it was, they would demand more to be done. They would say when they were driving up, they saw a boy whose hair wasn't shaved short enough. Or who hadn't tucked his shirt in. The angrier they were, the more we suffered."

"What was the worst thing that happened there?" Shayna asked, clasping her hands together and resting them on her knees. She was fighting the urge to fidget right out of her skin. She had hoped people would be willing to share their experiences, but she hadn't believed they actually would. "What was the worst thing you witnessed?"

"The iron," Greywolf said, and for the first time his voice faltered. "A boy, the name they gave him was Jacob. I could tell by the look in his eye he'd had enough. The day after the Hillderstaff brothers came, a supervisor named Conway was looking to hurt someone. Jacob was heard speaking our language to another boy and wouldn't go to the shack for his punishment. We were working in the laundry room. Conway plugged in the iron and burned him badly. All over his back. The smell and the screaming is something I will never forget."

"What happened to him after that?" Shayna asked, wincing, fearing the answer.

"I don't know," Greywolf admitted. "Jacob was taken away, and we never saw him again."

"What do you mean?" Shayna asked, leaning in and looking

at him intensely. "Where would they have taken him? Did he go home?"

"He had no home. His parents had been killed in an accident. There were ranks for all of us, like the military. The orphans never moved up in rank. They had to wear red handkerchiefs on their arms during the day. They were put in the most grueling jobs. They were the first to be beaten if something went wrong. I remember feeling lucky that my mother was still living, and I didn't have to be lumped in with them. Those were the ones who would go away and not come back."

"Did anyone ask where Jacob or the other missing boys were?" Shayna's voice had urgency she couldn't tamp down. It seemed logical that someone would question how a boy would be there one day and gone the next. She did however remember the stories Aponi had explained in shocking detail and realized speaking up would not have been an option.

"We said nothing," Greywolf admitted, his voice laced with shame. "I never had the courage to ask when a boy I knew would be taken away in the night. We all wanted to know, then one day I had my answer."

"What do you mean?" Shayna asked. "You know where they went?"

"I found them," he said, closing his eyes and placing a hand on his chest. "One night I decided I would run away. If you ran home, they would find you and punish your parents. They'd convinced most parents this was the only option for kids like us. Some parents believed the laws that were once in place for indigenous kids and these schools were still in existence. My mother believed HIBS was the best place for me. So I was going to run somewhere else. I knew about some train tracks ten or twelve miles away. I was strong and light-footed. I could get there in one night. I'd hop a train and never come back. No matter how bad the world was, it would be better than that place."

"How far did you get?" Shayna asked, knowing he obviously wasn't successful.

"About two miles from the school. I'm not sure I really believed I could get away, but somehow I had. Close to daybreak I went down a path in the brush and suddenly stumbled into a large hole. It was too dark to see much of anything, but something told me to wait. Wait for the sun to come up. Wait."

"Why stop?" Piper asked incredulously. "You were so close to freedom."

"It was a whisper in my ear," Greywolf explained flatly, as though this voice he heard was to be obeyed. "So I waited, and when the sun came up I saw the hole was a grave. It was freshly dug. And there were more holes scattered all around me, the dirt was turned over and obviously something was buried. Graves. Some fresh. Some old. None marked with anything of any significance. I sat in that hole and thought about every boy who'd been there one day and was gone the next. I thought about how most of them didn't have any family that would know they were gone. I thought of the pain that would come to their ancestors, knowing they'd been discarded without any of the traditions we follow. How their souls would be lost forever."

"You were certain all the missing boys were buried there?" Piper asked, logic taking over as she pressed for answers. "You were young. It was a long time ago. How can you be certain they were there? Maybe it was not what it looked like."

"I could hear them," Greywolf corrected, shaking his head. "I could hear them begging for peace. I knew they were there."

"What did you do?" Shayna asked, fearful Greywolf would need another break soon or maybe ask them to leave. She needed to know everything she could about the graves. Aponi had offered nothing, but he thought correctly that Greywolf would know more.

"I stood from the grave and decided I would not be one of

those boys in the dirt. I walked back to the school. It would only be a couple months until I'd be free to leave there without them chasing me. I would listen. I would watch. And then I would leave. And someday I would help the boys they buried."

"You did leave soon after?" Shayna pressed on, watching the energy drain from his face.

"I left and got a job at a shop in town. The Hillderstaff family put in a good word for you if you had graduated from their school. It was a sign you had been converted. All the savagery removed, enough for you to be trusted with a job. I didn't know what else to do so I took the job. I met my wife there. We were wed two months later. It's not that I forgot them. I always wanted —" Remorse seemed to fill his mouth and soak up the words like a sponge before he could finish.

"It's understandable," Piper interjected. "You aren't to blame for what happened. Starting your own life isn't a crime. Especially after what you endured. You deserve happiness."

"I had plans to do something. To fight them in some way. But a few months later my wife was pregnant. I knew I couldn't do anything without putting my family in danger. So we moved deep onto the reservation and began a life of quiet hiding. They wouldn't find me. They couldn't have my children. It would stop with me. And it did. My children were educated on the reservation and taught who they are, not robbed of it."

"You protected them," Piper said comfortingly. "They were lucky to have you."

"I always thought someone would find the bodies," Greywolf said in a faraway voice. "The school closed a few years after I left. I thought someone would say something."

"Aponi has," Shayna reminded him. "And now you have." She leaned over and clicked off the recorder. "Could you draw a map where you think you saw the graves?"

"I don't know," Greywolf sighed. "I don't know about any of

this. What can you prove? What can you really do? The years have moved on too quickly. I've lost my wife. My children are all happily married and living across the country. I have a peaceful life now. I've come to the end of it. Anything we do will bring a storm to my door."

"No," Shayna said, reaching across the small space between them and grabbing his hand. "I will bring the storm to their door."

CHAPTER 10

On the reservation, silence wasn't hard to come by. People knew thoughts needed to be cultivated in quiet the same way seeds needed sun to grow. Out in the rest of the world however, Shayna hadn't met many people who could sit in silence. Some people could hold out a minute or two but then they'd be compelled to discuss the weather or some other small talk. Piper, however, seemed fully equipped to ignore the social norms most people had been prisoner to.

The entire ride back to Shayna's house was in silence, and yet they were both comfortable. The radio was off. Phones put away. It wasn't until they turned onto the reservation that Shayna finally spoke.

"Not everyone needs the details," she croaked out nervously.

"I agree," Piper confirmed, glancing at Shayna with a look of understanding. "There will be a right time and place to talk about what Greywolf shared today. You'll know what to do and when to do it."

"That's an awful lot of confidence in me," Shayna scoffed, pushing her bangs off her forehead and tipping her head back dramatically. "I'm basically spending all my time second guessing myself. Who the hell do I think I am? These are millionaires with top notch lawyers. They know everyone. I don't know anyone. This is crazy to even consider, yet here I am telling Greywolf and Aponi how we're going to win this. I don't even know what *this* is."

"Absolutely," Piper agreed. "They are powerful people. They've been operating this way for generations. It sounds like Nicholas's grandfather and his brothers had an agenda, and they did everything they could to accomplish it."

"They were just taking part in the long-standing tradition of wiping us off the face of the earth. Kill the Indian, save the man. That's what they thought they were doing. We were savages and they were our saviors. To think they built a whole school on that idea. And all those people they hired. They either agreed, or were so complacent they sat back and watched them exterminate children, either by taking their lives or ruining them."

"And you will tell that story," Piper replied confidently. "Maybe only ten people will hear it. Or maybe ten thousand. Some will believe you. Some won't. Some will care. Some won't. You might take down their whole empire, or you might get yourself thrown in jail."

"This started off as reassuring." Shayna sighed, looking at Piper helplessly. "You're just reminding me how impossible this is."

Piper smiled, her dark eyes brightening as she gave Shayna her best advice. "I can't say if what you're doing will turn out right, but I can tell you what you are doing *is right*. Sometimes when we set out to do something, that's the only thing we have to hold on to. And I'm telling you that's enough for right now."

"I'm glad you were there today," she admitted, leaning her head against the car window and watching the world speed past. "Hearing it alone is a lot. I went to Aponi's thinking I knew what to expect, but I didn't have a clue what I would hear, or how different it would be sitting in front of someone and hearing it. It was a lot to take in."

"You're not alone," Piper promised. "Now let's figure out what we do next."

"I'm assuming we have to go break up a fist fight between my brother and Nicholas," Shayna joked as they pulled in the driveway. "We should start there."

"I don't know," Piper said, pointing over at the yard to the side of the tiny house. "I think we should give them a little more credit."

Shayna looked on in astonishment as Tao and Nicholas worked in unison, chopping and stacking wood. Frankie was sweeping the metal steps on the side of the house as if that might spruce the place up. A broom wouldn't make this place any better. A bulldozer would be better at that.

"Hey," Shayna said curiously as she hopped out of the car to get a better look at them all.

Tao hardly looked up as he swung the axe and split a log with one strike. "When Mom gets back she'll want to have a fire out here. She was getting low on wood."

"Yeah," Shayna said quietly. "She'll appreciate it. And Frankie, thanks for sweeping and cleaning up. My mom hasn't been able to do much on her own lately."

Tao held the axe on his shoulder and looked over at Frankie adoringly. "She did the whole house. Mom's going to really like it."

Frankie blushed brightly as she turned her head away and kept sweeping.

"Yuck," Piper said quietly so only Shayna could hear. "How do you stand the two of them together? Best friend and brother?"

Shayna looked over her shoulder and rolled her eyes. "They keep acting like they aren't in love. It's exhausting."

"What?" Frankie asked, clearly picking up on something secretive that might include her.

"Nothing," both Piper and Shayna called back with a playful laugh.

Frankie looked unconvinced but eager to know if Shayna and Piper had success on their trip. "How did it go?"

"Good," Shayna said with a shrug. "I need to figure out what to do next. I have two people willing to go on record, and they have similar stories. I found out today there is only one more person on the list who is still living. I think it's much more compelling to have three people willing to go on record and recount what they experienced."

"Shayna," Tao groaned and Frankie instinctively set the broom down and made her way to his side. "It's Dad's brother? Guy?"

"He was there. He has a story to tell. Look what it did to his life. Look at what it did to our father's life too." Shayna had a shaky pleading tone to her voice as she thought about her father experiencing any of the things the first two men had described.

Tao planted the axe into the stump and shook his head. "He did those things. We didn't have an easy childhood, and you don't see us blaming our bad choices on that. Guy is no better than our father was. Even after Dad died, Guy never came around. He's a drunk too. I hear stories about all the trouble he's gotten into. We don't need anyone in our lives like that."

Shayna felt her chest flood with anger. Tao wasn't the source, but he was about to be the target. "You don't know the whole story. That's the point. I want to. It doesn't mean I forgive him, but I am not going to stick my head in the sand and pretend HIBS didn't contribute to their problems."

"How about you understand the fact that Mom had to work two jobs. Maybe understand no matter how Mom used to try to convince us we were camping with lanterns in the living room because it was fun, the power was actually turned off. Guy is exactly like our dad, just two years older. Don't open that door up for him, Shayna. He's not going to walk through it."

"I don't need your permission to speak to my uncle," Shayna said, an edge to her voice that showed she was serious. There would be plenty of things standing in her way during this, she sure as hell wasn't going to let her brother be one of them.

Nicholas tossed down the piece of wood on his shoulder and spoke up. "Your uncle is not the only avenue for this either. Remember I have access to the storage facility where more of the school records might be. If you find the right things there, maybe it won't matter what people will go on record and say."

Dirt and sweat had matted to his shirt collar, and there were a few smudges on his cheeks. Shayna wondered if Nicholas had ever had a day of hard labor in his life. Their lives were polar opposites, but she was grateful for all he was doing to help, especially since this was far outside his norm.

Frankie was leaning affectionately close to Tao, looking at him then suddenly back to Nicholas. Shayna knew her well and the expression on her face was the one that always came before she went full mama bear status on someone. "Nicholas, you say you have access. What does that mean exactly? You think you can just walk in somewhere and take what you want? You're over simplifying all of this. Some documents can't make the case as well as people telling their story will."

Tao grunted his frustration. "Isn't that what they do? They take what they want when they want it and think that's the answer to everything."

"No," Nicholas countered, and it was clear he was trying to keep his cool. "I'm not saying I can swoop in and make this easy. But I know where they might have kept the school records, and I know how to get them. I don't necessarily have permission to be there, but I believe in what Shayna is doing, and I'm willing to help."

Piper strolled up casually as though she weren't about to ruin everything, but of course she was. "Shayna is already running from some breaking and entering charges. There's risk here and none of you are thinking clearly. I'm being as supportive as possible, but I'm not going to allow recklessness that has long lasting repercussions. Especially when there is no guarantee of anything worthwhile in the documents."

Nicholas used the back of his hand to wipe the sweat from his brow. "I can make it easy. We could probably go in the morning. I know how and when we can do it. I've been giving it a lot of thought. My whole family will be going to the mountains for spring break. I'm going to bail and tell them I have too much school work to deal with. That will give us some options."

"You're not hearing me," Piper said, raising a challenging brow at Nicholas. "This is going down the way I say. End of story."

Nicholas looked completely unfazed as he dismissed her demands. "I understand that everyone sent you out here thinking we need some kind of chaperone," he started, but Piper laughed so loud he snapped his mouth shut.

Piper was having none of it. "And I know you've probably spent most your life getting your way, but we're not talking about deciding which golf course to play. You think it's going to be like what you see on the movies? It's not. You are completely unprepared." Piper drew in a deep breath and rubbed at her temple.

"Aren't you like a social worker or something?" Nicholas asked, a thread of arrogance sewn in to each word. Even with the smudged dirt on his face he spoke as though he just strolled up in a crisp new suit.

"Boy," Piper said, leaning in and whispering so only he could hear her, "if you knew half of what I've done in my life you'd be getting into that car and driving as fast as you could to get away from me. If we've got to pick the best place for a ceviche dish or designer shoes, we'll ask you. If we need to break into a place and get some documents without getting caught, you do what I say. Now tell me what you know about it."

Nicholas cleared his throat and straightened his back. "I . . . uh, yeah," he choked out. "That's fine. It's an old office building where my family used to archive everything from all the different lines of business. We call it the bunker. My grandfather is neurotic about paperwork. He won't even let some of his companies go fully digital. He feels like anything can be compromised if you put it online. But a hard copy, you can control that. It's triple copies of everything. And multiple locations to house them. The bunker has everything."

"The bunker," Frankie said, glancing knowingly at Piper. "Sounds kind of ominous. If he's so neurotic, I'm sure it's not the kind of place we can just waltz into. There must be security."

Nicholas kicked at a few rocks under his dirty custom-made sneakers and nibbled anxiously at the inside of his cheek. "I've been there. I delivered many documents there when I was younger and worked a few summers for my uncles."

"How long ago?" Piper asked, moving out of the sun and toward the shade cast by the small house.

"Two years ago," Nicholas answered. "I remember the layout completely. And there was a room on the top floor where they kept all the really old documents. They called it the attic. A few times they'd talked about having me organize it, but my grandfather had always told them no, it wasn't necessary. He'd said he had personally set the attic up and knew where everything was."

Shayna made her way toward Frankie and took the broom to help. "So you're saying if we do find something up there, he'd know about it. He personally handled everything up there?"

Nicholas looked suddenly uncomfortable as though he'd been

76

trapped. "I think if there is anything to find, that's where it will be," he said, dodging the question.

Piper leaned against the house and groaned. "Then you and I will go," she said, jutting her chin out at Nicholas. "But we'll need more than what you remember from a couple years ago. A lot can change in that time. Especially if they believe people are looking into their history. I'll do some recon and make a plan."

"You really want to get busted for breaking and entering?" Frankie asked, looking sternly at Piper. "What would my dad say?"

"He'd say make sure you have a good plan and bail money. I'll have both before we set foot on their property. It'll take time, but we'll do it right or we won't do it at all. Now can we get out of this heat before I fall over?"

"There's cold water in the fridge," Tao called as they all moved toward the house.

"Frankie and I will grab some groceries. Any requests?" Everyone looked at Nicholas as though he'd have some sort of laundry list of gourmet foods he'd require.

"I'm good," he said, shrugging off their attention. "I'm aware you all think I'm this pretentious spoiled brat. But I can deal with anything. I don't need a five-star hotel to be happy."

"Good," Shayna said, holding the front door open for him to walk through, "because this place doesn't have any stars. It has a broken shower and some sleeping bags."

"Don't be too long," Piper said, pointing a finger at Frankie and Tao. "You're getting groceries not going on a date. I'm starving."

"We'll be back quick," Tao promised. "I'm worried I won't be around to talk my sister out of the next crazy thing she wants to do. Stay out of sight in case that cop is crazy enough to step on this land and come looking for you. Everyone is on the lookout and will let you know."

"Thanks," Shayna said, flashing a small peace offering of a smile at her brother. "I know I'll be safe here." She had believed at a very young age that the reservation was merely the soil of her life, that she would someday burst free of it and grow upward and away. Maybe her roots would always hold her here, but it would only be a place she could look back at from her new life. It was a yesterday, not a tomorrow.

Driving back today, seeing her brother in their childhood home, she could feel the safety and insulation fold in around her. Tao was well respected here, and if he asked for support in her protection, he'd get it. For years, the reservation had been a prison in her mind, holding her back from everything the world had to offer. Now she was grateful for the bars she could hide behind.

CHAPTER 11

The night was growing cool as the stars burst to life. Tao stoked the fire behind their house and brushed off some old plastic chairs for everyone.

Shayna slipped into a sweatshirt and stared at the flickering flames as they danced in the light breeze. "Thanks for making dinner, Frankie. The rest of us are about hopeless in the kitchen."

"No problem." She shrugged and grabbed a stick, poking at the hot embers of the fire. "I'd say it's impossible to be around my grandmother and not learn to cook, but well—Piper."

"Everyone loves to give me a hard time about my cooking," Piper laughed, "But you'll be glad for the rest of my skills this week, trust me."

"I know we will be," Shayna said, smiling at Piper warmly. "Thank you again for coming. I'm going to see my uncle tomorrow. Are you up for the ride?"

Before Piper could answer Tao was cutting in. "I'm going too. You hardly know him. You don't know what he's capable of now."

"Like what?" Frankie asked, looking nervous as she fiddled with the stick in her hand. "He wouldn't hurt them would he?"

Shayna snapped up from her chair and shook her head. "Of course he wouldn't. He's my family. It doesn't matter what he's doing with his life, he's not going to hurt me."

"Maybe he won't," Tao shrugged. "But that wouldn't stop him from manipulating you. He'll play right into your hand, and then when he gets what he wants, he'll be gone. It's all a game with him. It always has been."

Tao and Shayna had never seen eye to eye on many things. Her way of life had veered far away from his over the years. But nothing brought more hostility between them than talking about their father or his family.

Tao was a natural skeptic. Always believing the world and its agenda was not set up for him or their people. And history had proved him right. But Shayna hadn't drawn such a small circle around her life the way he had. She made a place for herself that encompassed different cultures, different societies, and in doing so found they had common threads running through them all. Other nations had suffered and history had seen repression and genocide. It didn't mean Tao was wrong about what their culture had endured and was still trying to withstand today. But when you looked through different prisms of experience, it left room for empathy. Understanding. Clarity. Maybe that was the reason she rooted for her uncle. Maybe that was the reason she wanted to expose what his generation had endured.

"If you go," Shayna said firmly, "all you will do is fight. He will never agree to talk to me if you are there reminding him of his faults."

"He won't agree to talk to you about these things unless there is something in it for him. What will you do when he asks for money? What if he wants to come back and stay for a while? He is not welcome here."

Piper raised a hand to quiet them both. The fire crackled loudly, and the logs settled into place as she looked back and forth between them. "I think we can handle it, Tao. Even if Shayna doesn't approach your uncle the same way you do, I can assure you I won't be easily manipulated. Whatever family problems you need to work out, won't be on the agenda. He either is willing to go on record and discuss what he experienced or he's not. Anything deeper than that we'll leave for another day."

"On record?" Tao scoffed. "My uncle can't be sober long enough to walk into a courtroom. Not to mention he probably has outstanding warrants he'd have to face. I've heard all the trouble he's been over the years. It always gets back to me."

"I've been thinking about that," Frankie interrupted. "My father was pretty adamant that any statute of limitations on these crimes would have passed. If they would be willing to testify, it might not matter. There's hope for a civil case, some mediation, or a settlement. My dad said he'd call us this week and let us know when he has a clearer picture of options."

Shayna grabbed a log and threw it into the fire, sending burning embers racing into the sky like wild animals fleeing predators. "I already know that. The justice I want won't be found in any kind of court."

Nicholas stared at Shayna's stoic profile, lit orange by the flames of the roaring fire. She could feel his worried glare raking over her. "What does that mean?"

"The lawyers. The red tape. The power. I can't beat them that way. Evidence we steal from them wouldn't be admissible. Victims on record, the lives they've lived since then, wouldn't be deemed reliable. Too many years have gone by." She tipped her head up and instantly missed the warmth of the flames heating her cheeks. The stars were brilliant in the night sky.

Nicholas had an urgency in his voice as he pressed for more. "You didn't answer my question. You aren't going to go all vigilante, are you?"

"My sister doesn't do vigilante," Tao bit back. "If you knew her at all you would realize that. She's not some savage."

"I wasn't implying she was," Nicholas countered, puffing out his chest. "You need to cool it with the accusations. I also have skin in this game. I'm all for finding the truth, but my family's involved too."

"Guys," Frankie said sternly, waving them off as she gestured to Shayna. "This isn't about either of you and your egos. Back off."

Shayna slid her hands into the pockets of her hooded sweatshirt and sat back in her chair. "Don't worry, Nicholas, I'm not looking to inflict the same pain on them that they did to the kids they were caring for. That wouldn't feel like justice to me."

Frankie shook her head in agreement. "You're right. There's really only one way to make an impact on them that would have a lasting effect. You have to go public. Very public."

"Right," Piper agreed. "We already know they pay people for their silence. If this goes through the courts or some kind of mediation, they'll keep it behind closed doors. There will be iron clad non-disclosure agreements. If anything, they'll have more protection than they did before you started."

"But," Tao said, wrinkling his brow with thought, "what kind of platform could you use that would be big enough to really out them? All we have is access to reservation media networks, and their reach is minimal. Who could you trust outside of that?"

Frankie paced around as they thought it over. "You'd have to find someone you could trust who wasn't in any way beholden to the Hillderstaff family."

Nicholas moved closer to Shayna and put an arm over her shoulder. She dipped her head down onto him and breathed in his familiar scent. She knew no one else around this fire liked him, but he had been loyal to her. He'd saved her one night and since then had been by her side. He was different from them, but why did that have to mean he was bad? "I think I can help with that. There's a journalist, someone I know would be impartial. Kevin Stone."

Frankie perked up. "I know him. He's lectured at my school. How do you know him?"

Nicholas dropped his arm from Shayna's shoulder and ran a hand over his hair. "He approached me a couple months ago, asking if I'd comment on a story about Uncle Jordy. There were some rumors he'd pulled some friends into a bad investment and then tried to cover it up. I didn't know anything about it, so I had nothing to comment. He gave me his card and told me if I heard anything and wanted to go on record, he'd take my call."

Tao was looking to Frankie for some kind of confirmation, and she obliged. "Kevin Stone has a reputation of being reliably unbiased and credible. He isn't on a mainstream news outlet anymore since he retired, but his social media following is huge. He probably has a bigger audience now than he did before retirement. He writes what he wants, when he wants. If I had to pick someone to tell this story, he'd be in the top ten."

Shayna didn't look as excited as everyone else. "I won't give someone half a story. I'm not going to tell him about a hunch or rumors he could have discovered himself. He's conduit, that's all. Until I know the story can't be dismissed or minimized, I don't hand anything over."

Piper grinned knowingly. "You want a slam dunk? Understandable, but risky, considering the charges against you. Hand him the most compelling story in the world, but if you take too long trying to build it, it may not solve your problems. It may make them worse."

"She doesn't care," Tao commented in a resigned voice.

"You're being such a hypocrite. These causes have been important to you all your life. I've always been a traitor to you, someone running from our people and our culture. You've never been shy about calling me out about it. Now that I'm here, trying to do something, you have to give me a hard time. Look at what they just did to Mom. They took away the medicine that can save her life. You should care."

Tao rolled his eyes at her. "I do care. I'm not going to stop until the world knows about it. I wish I could do all of that without worrying what your future is going to be. The one thing I could always count on was knowing you had a good life. I've given you hell over the years about your choices, but I always knew you'd have a good life. Now I'm not so sure. You have more to risk than I do. It should be me going up against these guys, not you."

Shayna tucked her long silky black hair behind her ears and stared at him fiercely. "Did you see the sun rise this morning?" A smile tugged at the corners of her mouth.

"No," Tao remarked, matching her grin, clearly hearing this question before. "I didn't see the sun come up this morning."

"And yet it was in the sky all day long without you seeing it rise."

"Mom's favorite line," Tao groaned, his face softening. "You sound just like her."

Shayna stood arrow straight and did her best to convince her brother. "You may have never seen me do something like this before. But I can. I will."

CHAPTER 12

"Do you always get your way?" Piper asked, pulling into the driveway of a dive bar with a broken neon sign. The gravel settled under the car tires as she parked in a spot by the door. "I didn't think your brother would actually let us come here without him."

Shayna thought on it for a minute. "I think if you'd have asked me six months ago, I'd have told you I hardly ever get my way. Everything was an uphill battle. Nothing came easy. Then my mother got sick and all this stuff came to light with the Hillderstaff family, and I realized how lucky I was before. I did get my way. I got to go to every school event I wanted to. I got new books. College. Travel. I had a healthy mother who, even when she annoyed me, always showed she loved me."

"You deserved those things," Piper corrected. "I've seen how hard you have worked over the years. I've seen the things you've done to help your family."

"I wonder what was it all for? Look at me now; I've been kicked out of school. I have warrants out for my arrest. I've disappointed my mother when she needs me the most. I am exactly like my father. I'm no better than his brother, who is probably sitting on a stool in there getting one sip closer to death."

"Take it from me," Piper replied with a heavy breath, "you'll find yourself in the same situation as someone like your dad, but it doesn't make you alike. It's what you do to get out of it that matters."

"Don't judge my uncle too harshly, please," Shayna pleaded, sounding like a child. "I don't know what shape he will be in. Tao said all the people on the reservation said this is where we'd find him. He's still my blood though. I still have hope for him."

"We're off the reservation," Piper reminded her, hopping out of the car tentatively. "We should try to be quick."

"If he does want to talk, I'll try to get him to leave the bar and go somewhere to talk to us."

"Just try to spot him quickly," Piper said, pulling open the rusty metal door and stepping inside. "I don't want to hang around here too long."

They made their way to the bartender, and Shayna scanned the room for her uncle. She hadn't wanted to admit that recognizing him might be tough. She'd invited him to nearly every local high school function she had over the years, but he never replied. There was absolutely no reason to believe he'd be glad to see her, but hope swelled inside her. This man was as close to her father as anyone could have been. Locked within him were the stories and memories that could give Shayna new insight into half of her DNA.

"Excuse me," she whispered to the bartender, then forced some confidence into her voice. "I'm looking for this man," she said, flashing the photograph she had of her uncle. It was over ten years old, but his features were distinct, and she felt confident if someone knew him they could recognize him in the old photograph.

The bartender's face was smooth as silk, and her eyes bright and happy. A complete contrast to her surroundings. She looked no more than a year or two older than Shayna. She squinted at the picture as she tossed a rag over her shoulder. "Guy," she said, her smile growing wider. "Of course. Who's looking for him?"

"I'm his niece," Shayna said quietly. "I need to find him."

"Shayna?" the bartender asked, her face bouncing back to her bubbly expression. "Oh, I see the resemblance now. You both have those sweet eyes."

"Sweet?" Shayna asked, twisting her face up in confusion. "I'm not sure I've heard him described that way before."

The bartender nodded her understanding. "I've heard he used to be a little rough when he drank. It's hard to picture him that way. The year I've known him, he's definitely sweet. Did you want me to call him and have him come by? I don't think he's expected here until he starts his shift in a few hours."

"He works here?" Shayna asked skeptically, hardly able to imagine her uncle holding down a job. Especially in a bar. Even more bizarre was the idea he might be sober.

"Not at the bar," she laughed and waved the idea off as crazy. "He drives. When someone has too much to drink he gives them a safe lift home. He's been doing it for a while. It's reduced the amount of trouble we've had, and I know he goes to a bunch of other places and offers his services there too. I can't imagine how many people he's kept out of trouble or how many lives he's saved."

"He's sober?" Shayna asked bluntly, a cold chill rolling up her spine. "I had just pictured him sitting on a stool in here, wasting his life away. I didn't think he was doing well."

"Don't look so disappointed," she laughed. "I'm Tilly. Why don't you have a seat, and I'll call him. He'll want to see you. He brags about you all the time. You're in college, right?"

"Uh, yeah," Shayna lied, too embarrassed to admit she'd been kicked out. "Spring break this week."

"He has this stack of pictures of you and your brother from when you were little. He shows them around to everyone and talks about how great you're doing. Tao is taking a real leadership role on the reservation. He's proud of that, too." Tilly grabbed her cell phone and indicated she'd be right back.

"What the hell?" Shayna whispered as Piper sat down in a stood and gently pushed Shaya into a seat.

"That's good news," Piper insisted. "Dealing with someone who's drunk was not on my list of fun activities for today. He's sober."

"Then why didn't he come around?" Shayna asked, an ache in her heart spreading like fire over desperately dry brush. "He's been this close all this time and hasn't reached out."

"Maybe he'll have his reasons," Piper offered in a gentle voice. "I've always found it's best to give people a chance to explain."

"Yeah," Shayna nodded, only half listening to Piper. "At least he's been talking about us. He's been thinking about us."

"That's a good sign," Piper said, trying to layer her voice with cheer. "No matter what comes of this, at least you'll be able to talk to family. That's always a good thing."

"It's always just been us," Shayna said, tapping her fingers anxiously on the bar. "Growing up without a dad, I always pictured some kind of stand-in. Someone to give me away at my wedding one day, and my mind always drifted to Uncle Guy. I've had these pictures, these few flashes of memories of how funny he was. A practical joker. But he never stepped up. He never stood in for my father in any way. It was always just my mother, trying to keep us together. She gave everything, and look what she's gotten in return."

"I know," Piper said sweetly. "She's so lucky."

"What?" Shayna snapped. "Lucky?"

"You said look at what she has gotten in return. She gave so much and ended up with a pair of kids who have a passion for what is right. A drive for justice well beyond their short years.

Take it from me, motherhood successes have nothing to do with where you live or what your own future might hold. We measure ourselves by the legacy we leave. I guarantee when she looks at her life, at what she's created in her children, she's fulfilled."

"I don't want to let her down," Shayna admitted, looking at the wall behind the bar and seeing her reflection in the cracked mirror that ran the length of the room. "I couldn't do anything without her and all she's done for me."

"I'm going to let you in on a little secret," Piper whispered. "You know how to touch your mother's heart and let her know how much her love and dedication has meant to you?"

"How?" Shayna asked, looking like some brilliance was about to be bestowed on her.

"First," Piper said, looking very serious, "you call her. Second, you say those words. Mothers—we look like complicated creatures. But really all we ever want to know is that regardless of where your life takes you, we matter to you."

"I can do that," Shayna said, pulling out her phone and looking at the two missed calls from her mother. "Once we're done here, I'll call. I've got a lot to thank her for."

CHAPTER 13

"Shayna?" Guy asked tentatively as he covered his heart with his hand. "I can't believe it's you. You look so much like my mother." He edged his way across the floor of the bar and kept blinking his eyes quickly as though Piper and Shayna might evaporate.

"Uncle Guyapi," Shayna said warmly, considering a hug but settling instead for an awkward handshake. "I'm sorry to make you drive out here. I was hoping we could talk. This is my friend Piper."

"Nice to meet you, Piper. I don't live far from here," Guy said, waving off the idea that this had been any trouble at all. "I'm happy we can talk." His round face and deep set eyes were exactly like every picture she'd seen of her father. His hair was graying, and his eyes were framed with small wrinkles that deepened when he smiled.

"Can we do it somewhere else maybe?" Shayna asked, whispering so she wouldn't offend anyone who might actually enjoy the dingy bar. "I need to get back on the reservation."

"Why?" Guy asked, clearly sensing the strategic way she'd worded the sentence. "Are you in some kind of trouble?"

"I, uh . . . I don't want to get into it here, but I will be safer on the reservation. Can we go to the fruit stand? Maybe get a smoothie?" She thought of all the days she sat on the wobbling benches outside the fruit stand and envied the other children. Some days they seemed to have it all. They got toppings on their smoothies. They had someone there with them to laugh with. Normally she'd sit there alone, studying something well above her grade level and sipping on a free cup of water.

"That sounds good," Guy said, still looking worried that Shayna might be in some kind of trouble. "I'll follow you there."

Shayna and Piper hopped in the car and weaved their way back onto the reservation toward one of the main roads to the little fruit stand. It was just a shack surrounded by

homemade tables loaded with brightly colored fruits and vegetables. Inside were the smoothie blenders and a cash register that was left open because it stuck when they closed it. Quirky and familiar, it was the perfect place to feel at ease. Shayna hoped it would have the same effect on Guy.

"I haven't been here in ages," Guy said, nervously tucking his hands into the pockets of his shorts. "I haven't been on reservation in a while except to drop people off when they need a ride."

"Tilly the bartender was telling us how you've been offering that service to people who have had too much to drink. That's admirable," Shayna said as she gestured over to a picnic table behind the shack, and Guy nervously took a seat.

"I do what I can to help," Guy said, clearing his throat. "I have plenty to make up for and not enough years left to do it all. But I do try."

"I'll get some drinks," Piper said, taking their orders and giving them some privacy.

"She's a friend?" Guy asked, lowering his voice and glancing over at Piper as she got in line for their drinks.

"She's like family," Shayna said, not sure if that would feel like an insult to Guy or not. But the truth was the truth. "I trust her."

"Why do you need to? What's going on?" He nibbled at his jagged thumbnail and glanced around as though something was about to happen.

"I've gotten myself into some trouble," Shayna admitted. "But the good news is you can help get me out of it."

"I can?" Guy asked, furrowing his bushy dark eyebrows together. "If I can, I certainly will. You are my brother's eldest daughter. I want you to have the best life you can even though . . ." his words trailed off as he dropped his head in sadness.

"Even though my father abandoned us and drank himself to death? Even though you nearly did the same?" Shayna's jammed highway of words finally broke free. There were so many speeches she'd practiced, so much scolding she'd imagined. But now as she sat beside the man who was the closest tie to her father's side of the family, she felt pity for him.

"I'm sober," Guy replied, but it wasn't a victorious statement. The shame on his face was unmistakable. "I have been for over a year and a half. Actually, five hundred ninety-two days."

"That's good, Uncle Guy," Shayna said, softening her voice. "I'm really glad for you. I don't want you to think I'm mad at you or anything. I know your life hasn't been easy. Just like my dad."

"What kind of trouble are you in?" Guy asked, shifting the subject back to her. "I don't have a very good reputation around these parts, but I do have a few folks who could help us out if we needed it. Did something happen at school?"

Shayna thought over all the things that had happened at school. She thought of how this started and whether she would ever see a day where it would be a distant memory. "I had a paper to write for school," she said, starting at the beginning. "It was just supposed to be this fluff article about our roots. Most kids hopped online, plugged in their information, and wrote stuff about their family tree."

"You have a very rich history," Guy said, starting to sound optimistic again. "Your paper would have been the best in the class; I'm sure of it."

"It wasn't just about your ancestry, but more specifically how education had impacted your family over the generations."

"Education," Guy said, his voice dropping down again.

"Yes," Shayna replied, examining his face to see if he'd already made the connection. "I knew my mother had gone to the community school on reservation. I had assumed my father had too."

"No," Guy said, looking all around as though he half expected the past to come from the brush and bite him. "He . . . uh, we both —that's not where he went to school."

"I know," Shayna said simply. "I started researching a little once I knew he went to HIBS. I was proud at first. The Hillder-staff family name is all over the university and hospitals. I thought maybe Dad had been to some prestigious school because he was special."

"Listen," Guy said, wringing his hands nervously. "The past, my past especially, is something I keep hidden for a reason. I don't look back, because behind me are just mistakes."

"I can understand," Shayna said, reaching out to calm him. "I know what happened there. I know how bad it was. That's exactly the reason I'm in trouble now."

"What do you mean?" Guy asked, putting his hand over hers. "What did you do?"

"At first I was only poking around online, and there was nothing about the school besides things that focused around the Hillderstaff family. Then I found a picture with some names under it in an article, and I recognized a few people. When I went to talk to them and asked about their time at the school, they slammed the door in my face. Finally I found someone who was willing to talk to me as long as it was off the record. He gave me a copy of a document that he signed years earlier. Something that kept him from speaking about what had happened to him."

"Shayna, this is a snake hole. And the only thing you'll get if you go down it is bitten. I think we should talk about something else."

"It's too late for that, Uncle Guy. I'm already in trouble. That man I was talking to told me about a list of students he knew about. When he signed the documents to stay quiet, there was a man with a list. He was told if he directed them to other people on the list, he'd be paid extra money. He said he played dumb and didn't give them any names, but the list had some very valuable information on it. It was in a lawyer's office, and I needed to get my hands on it."

"I don't think there is anything I can help you with," Guy cut in, waving his hands for her to stop talking. "I'm sure your mother can help you. She's always been able to sort things out for everyone."

"Normally you'd be right," Shayna agreed. "But right now she's in a hospital bed getting poison pumped into her arm to fight the cancer she's been diagnosed with. And the clinical trial she was in, the cutting-edge thing that offered her the best chance of survival, was stolen away from her by the Hillderstaff family."

"Cancer," he said with a gasp. "Oh, Shayna, I'm sorry."

"She's fighting," Shayna said, her eyes welling with tears. "But she deserves to be in the clinical trial she was originally approved for. They've already killed my father, don't let them do the same to my mother."

"What can I do?" Guy asked, looking more certain than before that he had no way of remedying this situation. "I can't help."

"People are coming forward," she said, clearing the tears from her eyes. "People are going on record and exposing the Hillderstaff family and their associates for what they did in their school. It was abuse. Possibly murder. You know that. You never signed the contract with them to stay quiet. So I'm asking you to go on record and tell me what you experienced there. What you saw. With enough voices this story can be told, and we can force them to right as many of their wrongs as possible."

"You can't imagine what you've started," Guy whispered, now looking paranoid about the motives of each person at the fruit stand. "There is only one way out of this for you. Give them back that list. Give them all the evidence you have against them, and swear you won't pursue it. Sign whatever they want you to, and put this behind you."

"I'm not stopping," Shayna replied confidently. "No matter what, I won't stop until people know what you and my father went through. Look at what it did to him. Your brother, your only brother, ruined by them."

"He put the bottle to his lips," Guy said, shaking his head in disagreement. "Just like I used to do. No one forced him."

"You don't think his life led him to it?" Shayna asked, her voice prickly with defensiveness. The narrative she'd been creating only worked if her uncle agreed that their problems were caused, or at least made much worse, by HIBS.

"I can't look back, Shayna," Guy apologized. "I hear what you're asking. I know why you are asking it, but if that is what you are here for, I can't help you. My sobriety is a fragile thing. Asking me to talk about my childhood, it could break me."

Shayna wanted to argue, but how could she? Her uncle was winning a hard-fought battle with addiction, and it was common sense to see a revisit to his past would be difficult, maybe even dangerous for him. "I don't know what to do then," Shayna admitted. "I have two people who have risked a lot to talk to me about what happened there. But everyone else is either dead or believes they are bound by legal documents to not divulge the truth. I believe they killed boys and buried them in unmarked graves. Do you believe that?"

"Please," Guy begged, covering his anguished face with his hands. "Please, I'll do anything else to help you, but don't make me relive that."

"You've done so much to help me over the years," Shayna ridiculed. "I could always count on you right? You've been sober all this time, and you didn't even come to see us. We are your brother's children. Why wouldn't you feel any sense of obligation to his memory? To us." Shayna was throwing jabs like a fighter in the ring. It wasn't fair. It wasn't so cut and dry. But damn it felt good in the moment. Guy was taking on the chin quite well and for that she was grateful.

"I was keeping a promise," Guy said, his head hanging low and his face still covered. "Your mother asked me to stay out of your lives. She believed it was the kindest thing I could do for you, and she was right. I'd have dragged you all down."

"Maybe when you were drinking, but if you're healed now why stay away? I know my mother would have welcomed you back. Especially now that she's sick."

"I don't trust myself," Guy admitted pitifully. "Today is a good day. Yesterday was too. Tomorrow: I never know about tomorrow. If I start coming around again, what will happen if I screw up?"

"I don't know," Shayna shrugged, hopping to her feet. "Just like I don't know what my life would be like if my father was alive. We don't know answers to questions like that."

"I want to be in your life, Shayna. I want to help your mother and your brother if I can. I'm sorry I didn't reach out sooner, but you're right, now is the time. There are things I can help with. I've started saving some money."

"We don't want your money," Shayna said, watching Piper

make her way back, balancing three drinks in her hand. "This is the last time I'll ask you, because I don't intend to beg. Will you help me take down the Hillderstaff family? Will you help me expose them and get my mother back in the clinical trial? Will you be brave?"

"No," Guy said flatly, his face exposed and his eyes fixed on her. "I won't get involved with something that will only make your troubles worse. You can't win, but you can run. I know some people who can help you get away from here. Tao too, if he wants."

"I'm done running," Shayna said, pulling his drink from Piper's hand and slamming it down on the table. "I'm done waiting too. Waiting around for people who share my blood to come and be a part of my life. Goodbye, Uncle Guy."

Luckily Piper read the situation correctly and didn't linger behind, asking questions. She casually poked the straw into her smoothie and started sipping away as though nothing awkward had happened. Shayna slammed the car door and sank into the front seat with an epic huff.

"So, he's a no?" Piper asked, offering Shayna her smoothie. "He may come around. It's a lot to consider when it comes out of the blue."

"He won't come around," Shayna grumbled. "He never has, and I don't expect him to start now. I don't need him anyway. Forget him. We're going to get those documents Nicholas has access to. We are going to find the graves. Even if we can't get more students to talk, this isn't over."

"Students," Piper said, lighting with an idea. "That's it."

"What?" Shayna asked, her heart still thudding against her chest as she boiled over with anger and disappointment.

"The students can't say anything but maybe some staff will. Some students held out and didn't sign the non-disclosure documents, so maybe some staff members did the same."

"The people who worked there witnessed unimaginable cruelty and did nothing. You think they are going to want to tell us anything?"

"I learned something about cold cases a few years ago. Loyalties shift. Marriages end. Friendships fall apart. Alibies don't stand the test of time. There are death bed confessions. Everyone thinks about how much evidence deteriorates over the years. But sometimes a case or a story can grow stronger when time passes."

"I guess," Shayna sighed. "I really wanted him to talk to me. I wanted to hear him say he hated the Hillderstaff family, and they destroyed his life."

Piper offered a knowing look. "Because that would mean they ruined your father's life too. There would be some real proof that had they not gone there he might still be alive today."

"Right," Shayna admitted. "I feel like there are two things going on here. I want the Hillderstaff family and their associates to be held accountable for the wide range of things they've done to hurt people. But I also want the personal satisfaction that will come from knowing what my dad experienced and how it was the cause of his dysfunction. Not—"

"Not you?" Piper asked, raising a questioning brow as the car idled in the parking lot of the fruit stand.

Shayna didn't answer, mulling over the idea. Before she could either accept or deny it, there was a small tap on her window. She rolled it down but didn't bother greeting her uncle with any kindness.

"Simon Coldwater," he said simply. "A boy who was in perfect health one day and buried the next. Rumor was he'd been caught with some beads from the res. He was singing a song of peace in our tongue. I thought he was an orphan, but turns out he wasn't. I heard years later his mother was putting up a stink, demanding answers."

"What about staff?" Piper asked, unwilling to miss the opportunity. "Who was sympathetic? Who spoke up to make it stop? There had to be someone who tried."

"Nurse Willis," Guy answered quickly. "Her first name was Syby or Cybil. I can't remember, but I know they fired her because she kept insisting the boys be sent to the hospital when they were injured badly. I heard one morning she threatened to expose the school for using excessive force on the children, and by that afternoon she was fired."

"And do you know what became of her?" Piper pressed on. "Did she stay in the area? Continue to work somewhere close by."

"No," Guy answered as though her question was completely foolish. "They ruined her. I don't know how but they had her nursing license revoked. I heard there were rumors flying around that she'd gotten pregnant while working at the school, but I never believed that. I heard she moved back with her parents. I think they lived in Benson. She always had a seashell bracelet on. She was very nice." The phone in his shirt pocket started ringing, and he fumbled for it. "I have to go to work. People need me for rides. I have to go."

"Thank you, Uncle Guy," Shayna said earnestly as he backed away from the car window and grabbed his car keys. "If anything changes, and you have more to say, please call me." She scratched down her phone number on a receipt and tucked it in his hand.

"Be careful," Guy begged. "If there comes a point where running is all there is left to do, run."

CHAPTER 14

"How is everyone holding up?" Michael asked, and Shayna could hear he was not alone. Everyone who usually crammed around the table for dinner was crowded around the speaker phone. In Shayna's tiny house, they'd organized every bit of information they could. Laptops were open and scraps of papers and notes were piled up.

"We're fine," Piper assured him, plastering a smile on her face even though he couldn't see it through the phone. "There's some good progress on our end."

"I wish I could say the same," Michael huffed. "I've consulted multiple people who specialize in class action and civil lawsuits of this magnitude. With the amount of time that has passed and the difficulty of gathering hard evidence, there's some precedence here, but none of it is all that promising for what you're trying to accomplish."

Shayna interrupted with a jolt forward to the phone. "I have a lead on the graves. I know the abuse and bad treatment can be hard to prove but the graves, the bodies will tell the story."

Michael cleared his throat and continued woefully. "There is precedence there too. Other similar cases of standard boarding schools and even church communities where unmarked graves were found and allegations were made didn't result in any kind of charges. The graves weren't even unearthed. The legal entity with jurisdiction might launch an investigation. That would mean interviewing all parties involved, looking for evidence, and even forensics around the school. But they have never ordered graves be disturbed if there is no actual evidence of murder or conspiracy to conceal deaths. It's likely they have records, real or not, that represent the causes of death. Anything remotely similar that I've been able to hunt down doesn't have a positive outcome."

"Dead bodies. Allegations of abuse backed up by multiple students. None of it will matter?" Shayna asked, choking on the words.

Michael continued as quickly as he could to try to calm her. "These cases aren't being tried in the court of law. People are writing books. They're doing podcasts and mainstream media interviews. But by the time they're ready to go public, they have a strong story to tell."

"That's fine," Shayna snipped back. "I will too. I already figured we wouldn't get the support of any court. It's never helped us in the past. I was naïve enough to think a bunch of graves might change that, but I should have known better."

"I know you're frustrated," Michael said. "It's completely reasonable to feel that way. It's crazy to think something like this can go unpunished, but I want you to be informed. Tell me what you have so far, and we'll come up with a plan."

Shayna was too angry to answer. She thought Michael would call back and say they had limited legal options, but her heart was hardly ready to hear it.

Piper leaned in and answered Michael. "Shayna recorded a powerful interview with a second former student. He drew a map to the area around the school property where he believes there might be some unmarked graves. We have a couple tips from

Shayna's uncle regarding a student who may have died under questionable circumstances. Also we are going to pursue some former staff who might be willing to talk about what they witnessed." She stopped short of telling Michael the potential for breaking and entering in order to secure more documents with Nicholas. Everyone in the room was looking at her as though they were now accomplices in withholding important information.

"It sounds like you're on the right track," Jules chimed in excitedly. "I hope you are all drinking enough water. You can get dehydrated pretty quickly."

"Yes, Mom," Frankie called. "We're all fine."

Shayna tried to pull them back to the issues at hand. "What do you know about Kevin Stone?"

"The reporter?" Michael clarified. "He'd be perfect for something like this, but I'm not sure I have any strings to pull with him."

"I do," Nicholas chimed in. "He has taken an interest in my family before and told me to reach out if I ever had anything to tell him. I think he'd be willing to get involved."

Michael hummed as he thought. "I agree. If he's someone who will take your call, I'd start with him. But like I said, you're going to be telling the story, trying the case in the court of public opinion versus a courtroom. That means you need compelling information. Credible and relatable witnesses. Documentation wherever possible. You need something people will not be able to poke holes in."

Bobby chimed in to offer some help. "Send me the names of any of the staff you're looking for, and I'll try to get some leads on their last known addresses."

"Thanks, Uncle Bobby," Frankie said. "That'll be a big help. There is one more thing I was hoping you could check out."

"Lay it on me," Bobby said. "I'm feeling left out, having to stay behind and cutting crust off sandwiches that the twins decide they don't want the second I finish. Next time I give you a hard time about this parenting thing, Piper, slap me."

"Deal," Piper answered happily. "That's the kind of promise I can keep. Now grab a pen and paper so Frankie can give you a to-do list."

"It's not that long," Frankie groaned. "But it might take some digging. Can you look into any archives or data bases that can identify any complaints lodged against HIBS? Dad, you must be looking into legal actions against them, but I'm thinking Uncle Bobby could see if there were any police reports or citations."

"Good idea," Shayna said, a wave of comfort passing over her. A room full of driven people could come up with brilliant ideas, and she was glad for that. "Anything you guys find send over."

Michael leaned in toward the phone. "We should talk about the charges against you, Shayna. I've done some digging, and the employee involved in the assault won't be backing down. He's a long-time employee of the Hillderstaff family and has worked at that particular facility for nearly two decades. If they are trying to silence you, it's safe to say this man will be loyal to their agenda."

"Yes," Shayna said, her heart fluttering with anxiety. "I can tell you I didn't shove him, and I didn't touch him. He slipped, grabbed for me, and fell. But there is no way they'd hold on to any tapes that show that."

"Probably not," Michael agreed. "But if we ask for them, they have to give us a reason they're not available, and we can use that to our advantage to create doubt. If they say the tapes were accidently destroyed, we can work with that."

Shayna closed her eyes and drew in a deep breath, "I don't want to think about that yet. I just want to build this story and get it in front of as many people as possible."

"This expose," Michael said gently, "things like this usually take months, sometimes years to put together. You're talking about days or weeks. To be able to pull that off effectively would be a miracle. You need solid statements from reliable sources and documents to support your story. You'll have to walk a fine line between urgency with the charges against you and not rushing the story so it falls apart."

"Sounds easy," Tao commented. "What happens when this story does hit? If there is no legal action that can be taken, how does it help Shayna or my mother?"

"It can be powerful," Michael explained. "When you publically expose the fact that your mother was removed from treatment as retaliation, it will correct itself. Public outcry. Plus, if you can come up with proof that they orchestrated that, legal action might be on the table."

"All we got was a letter," Tao replied flatly. "Some general letter in the mail saying my mother no longer could participate in the clinical study. No number to call. No more information."

"Send me a copy of the letter," Michael offered. "I'll get started on that too."

"Thank you." Shayna sighed. "I know you're all putting a lot of hours into this. You're without Piper and missing the week you had planned with Frankie. I feel terrible about it, but I'm so grateful."

Finally, probably after fidgeting and elbowing toward the phone, Betty spoke up. "These idiots messed with the wrong family. There isn't anything we'd rather be doing than helping you."

"Thanks, Betty." Shayna sighed with relief. "Everyone stay in touch. We'll send you everything you asked for and keep you posted."

A few final goodbyes passed between them before the line was disconnected.

Nicholas, who'd become quieter by the minute since arriving at Shayna's house, couldn't ignore the elephant in the room. "You didn't tell them about the bunker. Should I assume that's off?" He couldn't hide his annoyance.

"It's on the list," Piper replied, matching his tone. "It needs more research, but as you can see, there's no shortage of stuff to do."

"But you didn't say anything to them," Nicholas pressed. "It seems like you're dismissing my idea and focusing on what you want."

Piper crossed Shayna's small living room and eyed Nicholas closely. "There are times I look at you and I'm certain you're going to come out and say you're just kidding. But you never do."

"I know you think I'm a joke," Nicholas countered, but Piper wasn't having it.

"I'm not dismissing your ideas. Maybe you're used to being the smartest guy in the room. I'm sure we could fill this whole reservation with things you've learned in books I'll never know. But this is not your world anymore. So some of your ideas will be dismissed. Some will be put on the back burner. I suggest you find a way to accept that, because I'm not taking my time again to have this conversation. We're going to address the bunker when I know what we're dealing with."

"Yeah," Nicholas said, rolling his eyes and heading for the door. "I need a break. Shayna, I want to help you. You know I'd do anything to keep you safe; I just need some air." Nicholas headed out the door and into the setting sun. Another day done.

"Why do you let that kid stay around?" Tao asked, standing to watch Nicholas walk away from the house. "I thought for a while you were milking all this with him so you could get something on his family, but now I don't see it. Even if we get into the bunker and get something there is no way you could think he's trustworthy."

"Actually I do," Shayna shot back. "You don't know how I

met Nicholas or all he's done for me. You don't see what he's risking by hanging around with me."

"How did you meet?" Piper asked, her face showing sheer suspicion. "You keep eluding to some reason that we should all trust him. What's the reason?"

"It's personal," Shayna said, folding her arms across her chest defiantly. "I got into a bad situation, and Nicholas was there to get me out. The campus, it's a jungle."

"What happened?" Frankie asked, the only one brave enough to close in on Shayna and put a hand on her shoulder. "You know everyone in this room has your back. Let us in on what you see in Nicholas so we can see it too. The only way something like this works is if there is trust. Give us a reason to trust him."

"I did something stupid," Shayna admitted quietly. "I'm not one of those girls who gets drunk and makes dumb choices. I went to college to get a degree."

"We know that," Frankie comforted. "Trust me, this year on campus has been a lot to take in. I know how things just happen."

"You do?" Tao asked, sounding nervous, but Frankie waved him off.

"Just let her talk."

"I needed a ride one night. My car was acting up, and there was a book at the off-campus library I had to get. There was a group of guys who said they were heading to a pizza shop, and they'd give me a lift. I sort of knew them. A few of them had been in one of my classes. They were idiots, but I figured harmless idiots."

"What happened?" Tao asked, his chest rising and falling with angry breaths. "Tell me, did they do something to you?"

"They didn't," Shayna said firmly. "But that's because of Nicholas. I was in the car and when they flew past the library, I knew something was off. They pulled up to the pizza place and said I had to eat with them. A pretty Indian like me shouldn't go hungry. We could pretend it was like Thanksgiving. I told them to go to hell; I wouldn't eat with them, but they weren't taking no for an answer. They said it was the beginning of the night, and I'd be their date for as long as they wanted me. I wasn't going to stick around to find out what they meant. When I got out of the car they tried dragging me into the place, and Nicholas was there. I'd seen him around campus before, but I didn't really know him. I'd never heard of the Hillderstaff family besides their name being on plaques and stuff around school. He knew a few of the guys, and he told them to back off. They didn't want to, and he had to fight them long enough for me to get away."

"That was brave of him," Frankie said, as though she were encouraging Piper and Tao to agree. "I can see how that would bond you two."

"He didn't come into my life after he knew I was a threat to his family. He and I met first, and then this all started. The second I found out Dad and Uncle Guy had gone to HIBS Nicholas was there, supporting me every step of the way. As we found out more, I gave him every opportunity to talk me out of the next step. Early on, I wasn't sure I wanted to know the truth. He never wavered. Those guys started giving me a hard time on campus, and he made that stop. He may not be like the rest of us, but there is one thing that is the same. He's trying to help me."

"People . . ." Tao started, but then fumbled on his words. "People can be pulled in two directions, and it can be hard to sort that out. I've been there myself. Look at the reservation. There are days I can't imagine living anywhere else, doing anything besides working for the people here. Then other days I want to run and never look back. I want to start a life that doesn't have any of these problems. Nicholas might be a good guy who wants to help you, but you have to admit he must be torn."

"Sure," Shayna said, tossing up her hands. "Who wouldn't be?"

Tao spoke gently as he stared out the window. "At some point he'll have to choose. Maybe that fork in the road hasn't come yet. But you can't say you know which way he'll turn, can you?"

"I . . . uh." Shayna put a hand to her forehead and flopped back onto the couch. "I think he wouldn't have come this far just to change his mind."

"I think he likes you," Frankie said, trying to sound impartial but failing. "I see how he looks at you, and I know you pretty well. I don't see you looking back at him the same way. If part of his loyalty is based on the idea he thinks there might be something between you two, and that's not the case, this whole endeavor could hang in the balance. That's something you might want to sort out first."

Shayna looked at the door and realized how right her friend was. Nicholas had told Shayna exactly how he felt about her, and she'd continued to put him off, always saying things were too complicated while they sorted everything out. But it didn't matter how settled things were, she'd never look at Nicholas they way he did her. He'd been brave the night he helped her. He'd been kind and supportive ever since. It just wasn't enough. "How long until we can get into the bunker?" she asked Piper, and with the change of subject, she answered the question Frankie had asked.

"Three days at least," Piper said hesitantly. "I plan to go there in the morning and do a little poking around. I need to get the lay of the land. I should go on my own. It'll be easier. You guys can wait for the information to trickle in from Edenville. If I know them, they'll be working through the night on the stuff we gave them."

"I'm going to go talk to Nicholas," Shayna said, rising slowly to her feet and dragging herself toward the door. "He can't be wandering around here in the dark."

"Yeah," Tao said as she stepped outside. "Don't leave that boy in the dark anymore."

CHAPTER 15

Frankie and Tao had fallen asleep nestled together on the couch, surrounded by pertinent papers. Shayna had gotten up from her fitful sleep and watched the sun rise, painting the room with an orange hue. Nicholas had fallen asleep on a sleeping bag and was snoring as she looked over each of them, wondering what next week or next year would bring.

How in the world would Frankie and Tao ever make their love work? She'd be at school for another three years. He'd be doing endless work on the reservation. It wasn't as if she'd suddenly want to live here, or he'd miraculously solve every problem and be ready to leave. There was no logical reason for the two to believe they had a future that would work. Yet when Shayna watched them, it was impossible to ignore. Her brother would heed Frankie's *suggestions* of tactfulness and careful thought. Frankie, who had known only the world of Edenville, blossomed with the perspective Tao offered. Yet every time Shayna looked at them, she wanted to warn them. *Run. The odds are against your happiness.*

Her phone vibrated with a text message, and she was relieved to see Michael had already found something. The name her uncle provided matched up with something. She stepped out the front door and returned his call.

"Did you two sleep at all?" she asked as Michael answered in a gravelly voice. "I appreciate all the help, but I don't want you guys losing sleep over this."

"We're fine," he argued. "And this was worth it. I did some digging, and there were multiple inquiries about the school from family members about the deaths of their loved ones. Most went to the police that had jurisdiction. I was able to come up with seven. Six were dropped within days of being filed. No known reason for why."

"Who is the seventh?" Shayna asked hopefully.

"Your uncle was right. The mother of Simon Coldwater filed a report regarding her son's death at HIBS. He'd been sent to the school when his mother was ill and couldn't care for him. Then somewhere along the way he'd been listed as an orphan."

"That's the hallmark of the school," Shayna growled. "They preyed on the kids who had no one waiting for them at home."

"Simon's mother had repeatedly called the school when she recovered from her illness, but no one would give her any answers to where her son was. They told her he'd been sent to a farm to do some labor for a man who was teaching him a trade. Then she was told he'd run away and there was no longer anything the school could do to help her."

"So how did she learn of his death?" Shayna asked, trying to follow where the tangled web led.

"According to the report, she persisted," Michael explained. "She went to the school and demanded all the records they had on her son. She refused to leave. Eventually, a supervisor at the school took her into a room and told her there had been a mix-up with another student with a similar name. Her son, who was believed to be an orphan with no next of kin, had died. She begged for information about where he had been buried. There were ceremonies she needed performed on his body. In this report, they told her nothing. They weren't sure what had happened to his remains. They wouldn't even say how or when he had died."

"That's insane," Shayna gasped. "Cruel."

"From reading over the report, it seems as though the police did little to actually investigate. They went to the school and took a statement, which was redacted on the documents I found. There's a log of how many times Mrs. Coldwater went to the station or the school, demanding answers. She was threatened with arrest, yet she kept pressing. Then one day a few months after she filed the original complaint, it seems to have fizzled out. There were no more records of her coming in and asking for information. The good news for us: the case isn't labeled closed, but cold. If you can reach Mrs. Coldwater, and she still has interest in pursuing her son's death, you may have a path forward."

"Did Bobby have any luck locating her?" Shayna asked, feeling ready to slip on her shoes and run out the door if they told her where to go.

"No," Michael said regrettably. "But he did locate her other son. He would have been an infant at the time of his brother's death. I'll message you the phone number listed for him."

"Great," Shayna said, feeling a sense of victory, even though nothing tangible had come of it yet.

"Tread lightly," he warned. "We don't know why she suddenly stopped looking into his death. The other six people were likely given some form of payment and signed a document waving their rights in one way or another. But remember, there is no document that can keep someone quiet about murder. There is no statute of limitations. This could be something the Hillderstaff family cannot wiggle out of."

"Got it," Shayna assured him. "Thanks Michael. I don't know how I'd do any of this without your help."

"Want to pay me back?" Michael asked, through a laugh. "Keep an eye on my daughter and that brother of yours. I'm still getting used to her being a grown-up."

"You don't have anything to worry about. Somehow Frankie has turned my brother into a perfect gentleman. Having Piper lurking around every corner doesn't hurt either."

A quiet voice whispered from over her shoulder. "I wouldn't call it lurking," Piper teased, sending Shayna jumping.

"Yeah," Michael agreed, "You'll want to put a bell on her or something. She's stealthy. I'll send you the information I have and keep in touch."

Right after hanging up, Michael's text came through with the phone number for Kit Coldwater. After recapping everything for Piper, the others began to stir and groan at the uncomfortable sleep they'd muddled through.

"I have a lead," Shayna said brightly, trying to rally them all. "Piper is heading to the bunker with the information Nicholas gave her, and we're making a phone call."

"Coffee," Frankie grumbled, throwing her blanket off and stumbling toward the kitchen.

"Yeah," Nicholas agreed, still seeming pissed about the argument from last night. "I have some stuff I have to do today. Can I get a ride into town?"

"Sure," Tao offered, looking more than happy to get rid of Nicholas for a little while. "I'll get coffee on my way."

A few minutes later Piper waved goodbye and pulled out of the driveway; Tao and Nicholas weren't far behind. Frankie handed Shayna a mug of coffee as they stared at the wind-blown, barren land around the house.

"He's just looking out for you," Frankie said from behind her mug of coffee. "You know how difficult it is for Tao to express himself. He's worried."

"I know," Shayna said, drawing out the words dramatically. "It's not like I haven't given him reasons to worry. But I just realized this is our first chance alone. What is going on with you two? Are you dating? Is it serious? If I have to be in this weird position with best friend and brother romance, I want to be kept up to date."

Frankie flushed red and rolled her eyes. "Don't you have that important phone call to make?"

"It's too early. Nothing starts a call off on the wrong foot more than waking someone up. Stop changing the subject."

"Going back home last year was the right thing for me," Frankie explained. "I was here, being pulled back and forth between Tao and Maxwell, trying to decide my future. Then I realized I didn't have to decide. I could take a breath and think it over. When I was with my family I did a lot of thinking."

"And?"

"Most of it was about Tao. Logistically, nothing about our relationship will be easy, yet the only thing harder is not trying. We've talked on the phone all the time this past year. You know we've made a few trips to see each other. I feel like we've actually gotten to know one another in a very honest way. It's been slow, but it's been real."

"Is it going to stay slow?" Shayna asked, nudging Frankie with her elbow. "I have to report back to your family soon. They're anxiously awaiting. They like Tao a lot. I think they'd be happy for you."

"They can keep waiting, because anything I tell you stays between us," Frankie demanded, but it was an unnecessary request. Their friendship was rooted solidly in holding secrets. "When I close my eyes and think about my future, there is nothing I see clearer than

Tao. The problem is, he's all I can see. I can't picture where we'll be. How we'll make anything work. Neither one of us should have to compromise the most important things in our lives. He sees his future here on the reservation, driving change. That's one of the things I love about him. Every time we talk about the future I get a bad feeling in the pit of my stomach. I don't see how we can make it work."

"Do you think anyone really knows when they start out? I bet when my mom and dad got married they had a grand plan. I bet when Betty and Stan got married they knew what they wanted. Look at it now. Stan was killed on duty, and my father threw his life away. You have right now. If that means talking on the phone and visiting when you can, then so be it. When things change, life pushes you all over the place. There is no way to know what you'll have someday, but it doesn't mean you shouldn't embrace what you have right now."

"I'm scared," Frankie admitted, taking a long sip of her coffee. "I'm afraid to fall more in love with him for fear it won't work out."

"I'm finding fear is like oxygen. It's just life. I'm afraid my mother might die. I'm afraid I'll go to jail."

"Oh my gosh," Frankie said, dropping her head down, a curtain of her hair falling between them. "I'm being so ridiculous. These are petty things compared to what you're dealing with."

"No," Shayna said quickly, dismissing the idea. "You're trying to pick who will stand with you when big things happen. I can't tell you what you should do, but I think Tao is a good person to have around when the fear becomes real. It's important you know that."

They stood in silence, watching the occasional bird cut through the cloudless sky. The expanse of land before them stretched on and on. The sun blazed on their faces relentlessly. A new day was beginning.

"Let's make that phone call," Frankie said cheerfully. "I have a good feeling about it."

"If I fail," Shayna whispered, her feet frozen and her voice gravelly, "take care of my mother please."

"This is going to be—" Frankie started, but stopped when she saw the serious look on Shayna's face. "I will. I promise. No matter what happens I'll be there for your mother."

"That's what it's like to have someone around when the fear sets in. If Tao can be there for you like you both have been for me, then you'll be fine."

CHAPTER 16

The phone rang four times, and Shayna was certain it was going to voicemail. A raspy voice said hello a couple times before she realized it was her turn to talk.

"Um, yes. Is Kit Coldwater available?" Shayna asked, attempting to sound casual.

"No, he's not here. Can I take a message?" the voice on the other end of the line asked as though this was another casual call.

"Do you know when he'll be back?" Shayna pressed, trying to sound as professional as possible.

"About three to five years, according to the judge." The reply was laced with a little chuckle but Shayna was sure it wasn't a joke.

"He's in jail?" Shayna asked, deflating with disappointment. If he were some kind of criminal, his credibility as a witness could easily be called into question. "How could Michael have missed that?" she wondered out loud to Frankie.

"We're not buying anything you're selling. I need to get going."

"I'm not trying to sell you anything," Shayna shot out desperately. "My name is Shayna, and I live on the Tewapi Reservation. I was hoping for a chance to discuss something with Kit about his brother."

"What do you know about it?" the voice challenged, now defensive. "Kit's my father. He has nothing to say about his brother or anything else from back then."

"I'm looking for answers. May I have your name? I promise you I'm here to tell the real story. I hoped your uncle could talk to us about what happened to his brother. Why his mother stopped pursuing it at HIBS so suddenly. I know your father was only an infant when his brother died, but I'm wondering if he has any information that may help in an investigation. Can you please tell me your name?"

"Lincoln," he offered cautiously. "But I don't have anything to say to you. We're not going to get tricked again."

"Tricked?" Shayna asked, "Who tricked you?"

"They tricked my grandmother. The police told her if she stopped hounding them, they would get answers for her. They said to stop coming around and let HIBS think she'd moved on. Then they would put pressure on them."

"But that never happened?" Shayna asked, dying to turn her tape recorder on but knowing it would be a slimy thing to do without Lincoln's permission.

"Of course it never happened. She went to be with the spirits without knowing what happened to her son. My father went to prison because of this. What do you want with the past?"

Shayna immediately started direct questioning, knowing the window of opportunity could snap shut at any moment. "Did your grandmother find anything about what happened to your uncle? Where he was buried?"

"I'm done talking," Lincoln proclaimed. "You can't help us."

"I have a map drawn by a former student, leading to an area of land he remembers having unmarked graves. I have multiple former students willing to go on record and discuss the treatment at HIBS. Things are starting to happen. You can be a part of that."

"Yeah," Lincoln huffed. "I pick vegetables on a farm off reservation. I'm not going to be any help in this."

"You're his next of kin," Shayna countered. "The case on your uncle's death is still open. If you pursue it, they'd be compelled to look into it. You can tell them where the unmarked graves are. You can push to investigate his death. By all accounts he was a healthy fourteen-year-old boy. Something must have happened, and someone should be accountable."

The line was quiet for a long minute, and Shayna and Frankie held their breath, wondering if Lincoln had hung up.

"I want to meet you first," he said, sounding calmer. "You have to show me proof that what you are saying is true."

"I can," Shayna blurted. "I'm on the Tewapi reservation. I can meet anywhere you want, and I can show you. We're making a case against them, and I think your grandmother's tenacity is going to play a part in what we do."

"She hated giving in," Lincoln admitted solemnly. "She wanted to be the one to find the answers. It's one of my earliest memories, her talking about Uncle Simon."

Shayna closed her eyes and rested her hand over her heart. "My father was a student at HIBS. He survived but drank himself to death when I was very young. I know how a place like that can ruin a family. It's why I want to do this. Tell me when we can meet. I'll come to you if you aren't too far."

"I know where the Tewapi reservation is. I'll come to you. Text me a place to meet, and I'll be there."

"Today?" Shayna asked, wanting him to know she was serious. "We don't have much time to pull this together. The Hillderstaff family knows I'm pursuing this, and they want to silence me."

"I can come today," Lincoln said with a sigh. "I have some things my grandmother saved. Maybe they will help. You'll want to call Detective Lastly though. I'll text you his number. He works with the police department that has jurisdiction, and he is one of us."

Shayna understood that to mean he was indigenous. "And you trust him?" she asked tentatively. "It doesn't seem like he's done much to help you find the truth."

"His hands have been tied," Lincoln cut back quickly. "He's needed more to work with. You sound like you have something. If we give it to him, maybe we can get somewhere."

"Can he come with you today?" Shayna asked hopefully. "Like I said, we don't have much time. The more we can quickly pull together, the better. As a matter of fact, what if we meet where the graves are."

Frankie's back shot arrow straight as she tried to get Shayna's attention. They'd both agreed it would be better for her to stay quiet on the call, but this idea had clearly caused some concern.

"I'll text you the information," Shayna hurried. "Thank you again. I promise this will work out." After a quick goodbye, she disconnected the phone and tried to avoid Frankie's judgmental stare.

"Shayna," Frankie started, a look of astonishment on her face. "We can't just follow some handwritten map to what could end up being a crime scene. You're rushing this, and you're going to compromise what you're trying to do."

"I'm working against the clock," Shayna countered. "It's not like I have much time to work on it. They're going to arrest me. I can't put it off forever."

A car engine could be heard in the distance, and both girls jumped to their feet, pushing aside the lace curtains a fraction so they could peek outside. "It's just Tao," Shayna said, her hand resting over her thumping heart. "He must have just dropped Nicholas off in town somewhere."

"What do you think Nicholas had to do?" Frankie asked in a most leading way. Shayna understood that no one was convinced of where Nicholas's loyalty would fall when push came to shove.

"He probably needed to sort some stuff out with school," she explained, waving off the idea that it could be more than that.

"Are you telling Piper or Tao about meeting Lincoln and going to the school site to try to find the unmarked graves?" Frankie asked, raising a challenging brow at her friend. "I know you don't want to deal with the drama that comes from involving your brother in this, but I think having him around can be helpful."

"I know why you like having him around," Shayna teased as the car door slammed in the driveway.

"Stop avoiding the question," Frankie scolded. "You know I'll support anything you want to do. You've had my back a million times before, and you know I have yours. I just hope you can put the emotion aside for a little while and realize how much Tao can help."

The doorknob twisted, and Frankie held her breath, staring insistently at her friend. A little flicker of mischief broke across her face.

"Are you talking about me?" Tao asked as he stepped inside and glanced curiously between the two of them.

Shayna let Frankie hang there uncomfortably before finally speaking up. "We got in touch with someone from Simon Cold-water's family. We're going to meet him. Do you want to come?"

There was an audible sigh of relief from Frankie, who flopped down on the couch. "It's at the site where we believe the bodies might be buried outside the school."

"And we're meeting a detective there too," Shayna said, playfully self-assured. "You in?"

Tao looked back and forth between them as though he were waiting for the punch line. When they didn't break out laughing, he shrugged his shoulders. "When do we leave?"

CHAPTER 17

"Piper is going to kill us," Shayna said as she looked at the hand-drawn map again and then at the path in front of them. "I bet she's finished at the bunker, and any minute she's going to call our phones, looking for us."

"It's a little late to turn back," Tao whispered. "We need to find this place before the detective and the Coldwater kid get here, so we don't look like complete idiots when they show up. Let me see the map."

"You think I can't find it?" Shayna asked defensively as she evaded Tao's grab for the map.

"I've been tracking and navigating most my life. You're using GPS on your phone to figure out how to get to the closest mall." Tao used his advantage of height and long arms to snatch the paper away.

"I know," Shayna huffed, spinning away from him. "You haven't missed an opportunity to remind me what a disappointment I am. If I was as committed to our heritage and our people as you are, this would be solved by now."

"That's not what I said," Tao replied, looking instantly to

Frankie for some kind of support. She moved a few inches closer to Shayna and wouldn't meet his gaze. "You made your choices. I don't see why you would regret them now."

Frankie held up a hand to him, and he snapped his mouth shut. "You guys have to work this out, but not right now. Figure the map out. Don't forget why we're here."

"Yeah," Shayna snarled back at him. "I haven't forgotten my roots. Our people were buried here. No ceremony. No blessings. Their spirits are wandering. I want them to have peace as much as you do."

"I know," Tao agreed reluctantly. "I shouldn't have said that stuff about the mall. You know I'm good at this stuff, just let me help."

"Yeah," Shayna said, rolling her eyes. "You are."

"The only point of reference I can find is this rock structure. We need to try to stay off the school grounds. Most of the area is fenced, and even if it's infrequent, it's probably patrolled. So we'll have to approach this way." Tao ran his finger over the map and showed them the route they should take.

Moving with purpose, the three navigated the terrain and brush as quickly as possible. "This is the property line for the school," Tao said, motioning to their left. "According to Grey-wolf, the graves should be about fifty feet that way."

"I'm nervous," Frankie admitted. "It seems like we're disturbing something that hasn't been touched for a long time."

Shayna spoke in a hushed voice as she moved forward, Tao and Frankie trailing just behind her. "People need to know where their family was laid to rest. It's the right thing to do."

Tao cleared his throat and nervously stuttered out a question. "How will we know when we're there?"

Frankie tried to answer but was cut short by Shayna's sharp gasp as she came to an abrupt halt. As they moved into the small clearing, there was no mistaking they were in the right place. There were a couple dozen plots with stones laid at them. Round, smooth rocks all placed a few feet apart where plots of dirt either rose above or sank into the ground around it.

"I count twenty-six," Tao said, shaking his head in disbelief. "It's like they didn't even try. These are just rocks for headstones. Oh man, look." He pointed to a plot ten feet from them, and from it protruded something that could be bones.

Frankie gulped and took a few steps back. "I'll head back to the road and flag down Lincoln and the detective."

"No," Shayna said, looking to Tao to explain.

"They will already be nervous. You're not the welcoming committee they're expecting. I'll go back, and you two stay here. Just don't touch anything. If we're able to get people to listen this could be a crime scene. It'll be important that it's preserved."

"Just hurry up," Frankie stuttered out, looking spooked.

"Shayna listen for me," Tao said, punctuating it with a unique bird-like whistle. "Just like the old days."

"Yeah," Shayna said, biting nervously at her lip. When Tao rounded the rocks and disappeared, Frankie gave her a confused look.

"What does he mean, listen for him?"

Shayna stared straight ahead as she explained. "When we were little and we were on trails or doing something that might be dangerous, Tao would whistle like that to get my attention without getting the attention of anyone or anything else. I've been hearing that damn whistle since we were little kids."

"Why would he need it today?" Frankie asked, nervously looking over her shoulder. "What would you expect could go wrong?"

"If Lincoln or the detective he was talking about seem off in any way, he'll want us to know that. But I wouldn't worry."

"Yeah, standing in this graveyard alone while we wait to meet strangers. I'm sure it'll turn out fine."

"We're not alone," Shayna said, closing her eyes and drawing in a deep breath. "They are all with us. They want us to help." She waved her hand gently toward all the unmarked stones and spun her body, tipping her head toward the sky. She repeated, in an even more confident voice, "They want us to help."

CHAPTER 18

There had been no whistle to indicate a warning. Tao had simply called out to Shayna as he and two other men approached. The detective hid behind mirrored glasses and an uneasy scowl. His button-up white shirt was ringed with sweat and his large military boots were laced tightly. With flecks of gray at his temples, his hair was cut short and styled neatly.

Lincoln Coldwater was a different story entirely. He didn't have a stormy look in his eyes, but instead a boyish charm. Where many indigenous men she knew, including her brother, frequently wore a look of apprehension and distrust, Lincoln had a light around him. A peace. He hadn't sounded so on the phone, but there was something carefree about him.

"Yikes," the detective said, as he looked over the scene. "I guess you guys found something all right."

"I'm Shayna, and this is my friend, Frankie." She nodded her head and waited for one of them to speak up.

"I'm Detective Lastly. I'm friends with Lincoln and his family. So you think his uncle was killed at the school and buried here?" He pointed to each grave and whispered out loud as he tallied them.

"We don't know that," Shayna explained hesitantly. "We know the school had multiple deaths and may have conspired to keep the causes under wraps. You're familiar with Simon Coldwater's case?"

"Very," Lastly answered proudly. "I've wanted to help the Coldwaters for some time, but I didn't think we had enough to go on. I had heard rumors he was only one of many deaths here, but no one would talk to me."

Lincoln cleared his throat and kept his eyes focused on the graves. "She says people are talking to her. She has things that can help."

"I do," Shayna said, digging the list out of her pocket. "I found this. It's a list of students who had died at the school, died after, signed a non-disclosure agreement not to talk about their time at the school, or none of the above."

"So you tried to get to the 'none of the above'," Detective Lastly said, nodding his approval of that process of elimination. "That's pretty good. That would have helped me. Most people just slammed the door in my face, and I was never sure why. Makes sense."

"What do we do now?" Lincoln asked, bouncing with nervous energy. "I want to know if he's here. I want to know how he died. The answers would be right here."

"Hold up," Detective Lastly said in a half chuckle. "Don't go getting your shovels just yet. I need a little more before I can have a team out here, treating this like a crime scene. This is a graveyard. Yes, people are buried here, but that's not a reason to exhume anyone. To justify the expense of something like that, we'll need real proof for a judge to sign an order."

"I'm working on that," Shayna asserted. "I may have someone who knows more than they are saying about Simon Coldwater's death. I'm going to try to get a statement from him."

Detective Lastly sighed. "It can't be hearsay. He'd have to have witnessed the boy's death."

"What if you can't prove murder?" Tao cut in. "Conspiracy, some kind of cover-up, couldn't that be prosecuted? What if they intentionally tried to keep the information from the next of kin, or if they tried to cover up neglect?"

"I'm no lawyer," Lastly said as he shrugged. "But I can tell you something like this, with the players you're talking about, can stay buried unless you give me something significant to work with. I'm talking real evidence."

Lincoln's voice boomed to life. "The proof could be right under our feet. You're basically saying we can't dig them up and get the answers, and our hands are tied if we don't. That's crazy. That's the reason my family have gone to their graves with no help and no answers." The passion in his voice nearly brought Shayna to her knees. There was so much pain in his words; she could practically walk over and hold it in her hands. "Before today we had no idea what had happened to the bodies. Now we know."

"It's not that simple," Detective Lastly countered. "I've been working on it."

Lincoln looked unimpressed. "Look at what she's done," he said, gesturing to Shayna. "She had people talk to her. Here we are, with an actual starting place. And she says she's not done yet."

Shayna dropped her eyes to the dirt as everyone turned her way. "I can't go into much detail. I have some stuff in the works. But I'll be honest, I thought finding this would give us more leverage. I mean, Lincoln is right. We could have what we need right here. Odds are these are our people. They're buried in their ways, not ours. That alone should be enough to get involved. We should feel pressure to give them the peace their families would want."

"I feel plenty of pressure," Detective Lastly countered now with anger. "Trust me. I knew Lincoln's grandmother when I was a boy. She practically raised me. Her dying without answers . . . I feel the weight of that every day. But it does me no good to tell you something that isn't true. They're going to make this hard, and the law will be on their side unless you have more proof. And don't even think about disturbing anything here. There's not a better way to get yourselves in trouble and ruin the case. Just let me do a little leg work on my end to see what our options are. I don't want to ask anyone I don't trust. It'll take a little time."

"I can't believe we're going to leave them here," Lincoln choked out. "I'm not. I'm going to camp out here. I'm staying."

"Don't be foolish," Lastly said. "You've got your job to think about. I'm not entirely sure if we're off the land owned by the Hillderstaff family. If they find out you're here, they'll have you arrested for trespassing."

Shayna interjected, knowing it wouldn't be popular, "I think it's a great idea. Someone should stay here until we have answers."

"I'll document with pictures," Frankie offered and waited until Shayna gave her little nod that it was all right.

Tao moved closer to Lincoln, who was maybe a couple years older. "I can bring you back some gear and supplies."

"If you're all going to be reckless," Lastly groaned, "maybe I can't help you. I'm not going to break the law. I'm sympathetic to the cause, you know I am, but I took an oath."

Lincoln, looking moderately calmer, replied flatly, "I'm not going to put you in that position. But I believe my uncle is buried here, and I'm not going to leave until I can take him home."

Lastly grunted and turned toward the direction they'd come from. "Stubborn, just like your grandmother. I'll start asking around to see what we can do. Any strings I can pull . . . you better believe I'll be tugging the hell out of them."

"Thanks," Lincoln offered uncomfortably as he brushed dirt off his T-shirt. "I appreciate what you guys are doing. I want to be able to bury him with my grandmother."

Shayna leaned in and touched his arm gently. "We'll do what we can. I promise."

Tao interrupted the intimacy with a slap to Lincoln's broad back. "I'll be back in a couple hours with everything you need to set up camp."

"I can't hear any more of this," Lastly said, sticking his fingers in his ears like a child and backing away from them all. "Call me if anything changes."

"You're really going to stay here?" Frankie asked, sidling up to Tao and slipping her arm into his. "By yourself?"

Tao chuckled. "She doesn't do much camping."

"Not at places like this," Frankie admitted. "What if the police come? It could be private property."

"Let them come," Lincoln said coolly. "I'll make sure the news knows exactly why I've been arrested."

"Sounds like you," Tao said, jutting his chin out at Shayna. "Willing to risk it all for something no one else seems to care about."

Shayna couldn't reply as she fought the heat of embarrassment rolling up her back.

"It's nice not to be alone in this," Lincoln admitted, though he looked reluctant to do so. He pursed his lips and seemed to think his words over carefully. "I don't know how so many people can have family who came to this stupid school and hardly any of them have anything to say about it. There would be no amount of money that would keep me quiet."

Shayna mustered a response, knowing she'd shared the exact same thoughts since finding out about this. "People are talking now. Some of them. We wouldn't be standing right here otherwise. I don't know if it was ever about the money for most people. Some were tricked. Others were threatened. Everyone I spoke with, who had signed the documents that forced them to stay quiet, were terrified. It took a lot for them to share the most basic information with me."

"Let's go back to the house and get supplies," Tao suggested as he and Frankie laced their hands together and made a move for the path.

"I'm going to stay," Shayna said, the words half question/half statement. "It won't take you long to get everything and come back. I want to talk with Lincoln more."

Tao's eyes went wide as though she had said something completely insane. "I'm not going to leave you here with someone we met five minutes ago. If you want to talk to him, we'll come back with the gear and stay for a while."

"I'm one of the few people who have stood here," Lincoln said, looking at the hallowed ground, "who isn't a monster you need to worry about."

Tao shook his head and cocked a skeptical brow at both of them. "Listen, this is not some macho brother thing I'm doing here. It's just not a smart thing to do. You're emotional now; you're not thinking clearly."

Frankie let out an enormous cackle of a laugh. "Sometime I wonder how you make it through a day without getting slapped in the face. I actually agree with you, but the way you're making your case sounds like a chauvinist idiot."

"But you agree," Tao said, pointing a finger at Frankie and putting her on the spot. "She should come back later."

Frankie looked at Shayna with a gentle smile. "If it was the other way around, she'd drag me kicking and screaming out of here for my own good. Lincoln, I'm sure you're a wonderful guy, but there's more at play here than that. Shayna, you are safest on the reservation, not sitting outside the property of the people who are trying to bring you down."

Shayna opened her mouth to offer some logical rebuttal, but she had none. They were both right. "I want to come back this evening," she insisted. "Lincoln, you said you had some things to share with me about all this."

"I do," he said, "I wanted to see if you were someone I could trust before I told you anything more."

"You can trust us," Shayna promised, looking earnestly up at him. "I want what you want."

Lincoln let his eyes linger on her face for a few extra beats as he seemed to decide. "My grandmother recorded every conversation she had about my uncle. She had this little tape recorder, and after the first time she went to the school and he wasn't there, she taped everything. My dad used to tell her she was crazy. But I've listened to every second of those tapes. They aren't great quality, but I can make almost all of it out. She caught them red-handed multiple times, lying to her and changing their story. I don't know how much of it can actually help, but she worked hard, she fought hard."

"I bet she did," Shayna comforted. "People knew that. One source gave me your uncle's name, and the report the police have has notes about your grandmother's tenacity."

"Your brother and friend are probably right," Lincoln said quietly. "If you're already on their radar, it would be better to come back later when it's dark. I have some water. I can wait until then."

"Yeah," Shayna finally conceded, knowing it wasn't logical to sit in this graveyard with a stranger. Lincoln didn't feel like someone she'd just met, more like someone she could understand pretty quickly. She saw a piece of her pain in his expression when he realized finding the bodies wasn't enough. "We will be back. You can count on that."

"Sure," Lincoln said, finding a shady spot by a rock formation. "I'm sure your word is good."

With that, Frankie tugged at Shayna's arm and headed down the path toward their car. It would be a long walk, and it felt like they were carrying the weight of the world on their shoulders.

"How can that not be enough?" Tao exploded as they reached the car, and he crammed the key in the ignition.

Frankie went into logical explanation mode, just as her father would have. "There's no law that says when someone dies of natural causes you have to have them buried in any certain way. There has to be some kind of complaint filed with evidence. If those boys all died of a flu outbreak, for example, the school was well within its legal rights to bury them."

"Frankie," Shayna said flatly. "It's not right."

Looking horrified, Frankie's cheeks flushed red. "Of course it's not right," she said adamantly. "It's horrific. It's a moral abomination to bury children in a way that doesn't match that person's beliefs and traditions. It's disgusting to think their parents or relatives weren't notified."

"Sorry," Shayna apologized, hanging her head. "I'm just disappointed. I keep thinking the next thing is going to be the one that unlocks this story. But it's never enough."

Frankie perked up a little as she replied, "No one thing is going to be enough. It's like a mosaic. All the small pieces don't look like much until you put them together and step back. You're going to build something, Shayna, something people can't ignore."

Tao put the car in reverse and pulled onto the road. "I hate to say it, Frankie, but you'd be amazed what people are willing to ignore when it doesn't affect them."

Frankie's phone rang, and she groaned at the name on the screen. "Piper is calling. She's going to kill us."

"I'll take the heat for this one," Tao said gently. "Most people expect me to be in trouble. I hate to let them down."

"No," Shayna said, shaking her head. "This is on me. She's

not going to like the idea of us coming back tonight either. So let me talk with her and try to get her to understand."

"Piper is very understanding," Frankie said optimistically. "She can see how important this is. If you level with her, she'll understand."

"We're really going to do this," Shayna said, still bowled over at how her life had changed and how she'd likely never go back to the way things were before. It was like an injury. A bone could be repaired. Skin could heal. But she'd be forever changed.

CHAPTER 19

Piper and Nicholas sat on the front steps, unease painted on their faces. "We should have called," Frankie announced immediately as she jumped out of the car. "It all happened so quickly, and we didn't want to miss our opportunity."

"I'm sure," Piper said, taking a quick inventory to make sure all were safe. "Hopefully you ended up with a better outcome than I did."

"Did you get caught?" Shayna asked nervously. The idea of Piper in trouble made her stomach lurch and roll.

"Of course not," Piper replied coolly. "But they do have layers of security that won't be easy to bypass. Nicholas has some ideas. We'll keep working on it."

"We found the gravesite," Shayna said, her eyes locked on Nicholas as she waited for a reaction. His face flashed with shock then quickly morphed into excitement.

"That's great," he said too loudly to sound genuine. "I had no idea you were going there today."

"Where did you go?" Tao asked accusingly.

"I had to deal with a few things," Nicholas said smugly, clearly not intending to add more.

"What's that even mean?" Tao called back. "Because from where I'm sitting, you could have easily tipped your family off to everything going on. The element of surprise is the one thing we have to work with. They might know Shayna has that list of students, but they don't know we've found the gravesite yet."

"Why would I tell you about the bunker and the documents there if I was going to tell my family your plans?" Nicholas shot to his feet and dusted off the back of his pants.

"It's called a trap," Tao said in a cocky tone. "It would make perfect sense if you were trying to set us up. This way they'd know when we were coming, and they'd be waiting."

Shayna put a hand on Tao's chest to stop him. "There's no way Nicholas would do that. It's not a trap."

Piper put a hand to her forehead and quieted them all. "Enough of all of this. Listen, I'm happy to be here, but the squabbling ends now. You guys took a huge risk today, and that's going to be the last one you don't run by me first. Or this is over. I'm not here to be your chaperone or your buddy. I'm here because this herculean task you're taking on is way beyond what you should be doing on your own. You're emotional. It's personal. It's going to get messy. We regroup right now."

Frankie tried to protest or explain, but Piper wasn't having it. "Don't bother telling me how spur of the moment it was. We're moving forward. Everyone get inside. Pour some lemonade and start talking. I want every detail of what happened today.

"We're going back tonight," Shayna explained, busying herself with the important task of chipping off the remnants of her nail polish.

"To the gravesite?" Piper asked, raising her brows in surprise. "I'm not going through the list of reasons why that's a bad idea. Do you have to go back?"

Tao opened the trunk of his car and tossed in a few things that were leaning against the side of the house. "Lincoln is the nephew of Simon Coldwater, who might be buried there. He answered the phone when Shayna called this morning. We met him there. He wants to camp out at the site. He believes his uncle is buried there and won't leave until he gets answers. I told him I'd bring him back supplies."

Piper looked unimpressed with that explanation. "So that sounds like a one-man job. I don't think all three of you need to trek back there."

"Four," Nicholas corrected. "I'm going too."

"No," Shayna said, attempting to make her voice level and unemotional. "Just Tao and I will go. I want to talk to Lincoln. I think he'll let me record our conversation. If you heard how passionate he was, how compelling he spoke, you'd understand. But he doesn't want to be around too many people. We won't stay long."

Piper crinkled her nose as she considered it. "An hour," she announced, pointing a finger at the two of them. "You stay no more than an hour, and you answer your phone if I call, no matter what you're in the middle of."

"Absolutely," Shayna agreed quickly. "We can do that."

Piper paced as she wrestled with the challenges ahead. "This is going to get messy. You shouldn't have taken Lincoln there today."

Tao nodded his head in agreement. "And you haven't even heard about the detective who came with him."

"In. The. House. Now." Piper pointed at the door and gave each of them an unwavering stern look. "I can't believe I volunteered. I'm getting too old for this."

Frankie put an arm over her shoulder and affectionately kissed her cheek. "You love this stuff," she challenged. "If you were home right now you'd be sitting around, waiting for a phone call from us, dying to hear what we were up to."

"Maybe," Piper sighed, "but at least then I could have my nervous breakdown in my own house."

CHAPTER 20

Following closely behind Tao, Shayna kept the beam of her flashlight pointed by their feet. The air had grown cool and the night was quiet all around them. Tao whistled out a bird call, and a moment later a similar sound echoed back to them.

"We're not staying long," Tao hissed in a low voice. "Piper is right. You need to be on the reservation. I got two calls yesterday about people who have seen the poster of you. There's a reward now."

"No one is going to sell me out for any amount of money. They respect you too much. I can't walk around here without hearing about all the things you've done. The community gardens you started are feeding families, and they are selling the extra at the off reservation farmers market. The blog and newsletter are getting traction; you're giving people a voice. The mental health initiative. You're doing real things to change people's lives."

"I wish it wouldn't sound like that's disappointing to you," Tao said, giving her a sideways glance as she hurried to keep up with him.

"I'm proud," she corrected, tipping her head up. "I'm jealous. All the things I did over the years, I feel I was playing pretend.

Like a little girl marching around the house in her mom's high heels. For all the travel, all the trophies and scholarships, I haven't actually *done anything.*"

"You made friends with good people," Tao offered, but it fell flat against the feelings of failure Shayna had stacked up around herself. "If you hadn't done that, I wouldn't have met Frankie. The only reason I'm on the path I'm on is her." He whistled again and a moment later, the noise repeated back to them.

"Lincoln seems all right?" Shayna asked, depending on her brother's astute, yet sometimes critical, assessment of people.

"I don't think many people our age give a crap about a dead uncle they never met. He obviously feels strongly about it. He's willing to sleep in the dirt, risk his job. Frankly, he sounds like you."

"Committed," Shayna said, nodding her head in agreement.

"I'm thinking more like crazy."

They approached the site quietly, and Shayna adjusted the sleeping bag she had tucked under one arm. It was slippery and awkward to hold, even rolled up. But Tao had strapped everything else to his back, so she thought she should carry at least one thing.

"Sorry we didn't get back before sunset," Tao apologized as he wriggled out of his backpack and dropped it by Lincoln's feet. "You have everything you need in there for at least a few days."

"Thanks," Lincoln said, hesitantly taking the sleeping bag from Shayna and looking away nervously.

She realized the situation had settled, and the idea of camping out might not be realistic. "You know you don't have to stay here. I know you were upset earlier. Don't feel like just because you said you wanted to before that you have to now."

"It'll take a bulldozer to push me out of here," Lincoln replied, tipping his chin up proudly. "You have no idea what this has done to my family over the years. I don't think the truth is going to fix everything, but I sure as hell am not going to get this close and then give up."

"Us neither," Shayna said brightly.

"Damn," Tao groaned. "I forgot the two canteens in the car. Shayna, let's double back and grab them."

"You go," she said, studying the features of Lincoln's face under the moonlight. "We're good."

Tao opened his mouth to protest but threw up his hands and huffed. "I'll be right back."

"Are you hungry?" Shayna asked, crouching down and pulling some supplies out of the bag. "We weren't sure what you liked, so I packed a bunch of stuff."

"I'm not really hungry," Lincoln replied flatly as he started making a fire. "I'll keep this small so no one spots it. There are some camping sites about four miles north of here. A little smoke over this way wouldn't be too out of place."

"Good," Shayna said, suddenly realizing she wasn't sure exactly what they'd talk about. "So would you mind if I record our conversation?"

"I guess not." Lincoln shrugged. "I don't know what I can tell you that other people haven't already. You said you read the police report, right?"

"Yes," she said cautiously, "But I think the police report is impersonal and doesn't really depict how deeply it impacted your family. Can you take me through the story as you know it?" She clicked on the recording device and placed it between them as the fire took hold and the small flames began to dance.

"Uh," he stumbled nervously. "Where do I start?"

"Tell me your earliest memory of learning about Uncle Simon and what happened to him," she prompted.

"I was with my grandmother; maybe I was seven or so. We were sitting at the police station, and I remember the bench was really hard. I was complaining about being hungry, and she kept telling me we had to wait a little longer. It felt like hundreds of people had walked by us, and every time one passed I could feel my grandmother perk up, like this would be the one to help us. When someone finally called her name, I begged her not to follow the man. He had a scarred face and looked really angry with us."

"This was a police officer?" Shayna clarified.

"Yes. He led us to a back room and took out a notebook. My grandmother stood there and recounted the story of how her son had been killed at school, and no one had any information. I remember her saying she shouldn't have to repeat all of this. She'd been there dozens of times before and had already given statements. She wanted something done. She wanted Simon found. That was the first day I saw my grandmother cry." His faced washed with pain as he hesitated. "No, she sobbed."

"What did the officer do?"

"Nothing." Lincoln laughed. "He sat there. I remember holding her hand and wondering why the man kept sitting there, writing in his pad on his lap. When we finally left he walked us out, and I'll never forget looking at the pad under his arm and seeing some doodles he drew. He wasn't even writing down what she said. I knew then these people didn't care. They never would."

"What did your grandmother tell you happened to your uncle?" Shayna pressed. "How much did you know?"

"On the drive home she told me everything. She'd fallen off a truck at work and hurt her back badly. For a while they didn't think she'd ever walk again. My uncle was a young boy and my grandmother didn't have anyone to care for him. Someone from HIBS came to the hospital and convinced her they'd care for him while she recovered. They had pamphlets showing all these happy kids playing and learning. I'll never forget the look on my grandmother's face when she admitted she'd never forgive herself for the choice she made that day. If I had been older, if I had understood more, I'd have told her she had no other choice. She did what she thought was best for him."

"How long was he at HIBS?"

"He was nine years old at the time; he died when he was fourteen, or so they say. That's when my grandmother began demanding answers."

"Did she have any communication with him over those years?" Shayna asked, trying not to seem as though she were judging.

"She tried. But she often heard from the school that Simon was thriving, and if he began talking to her on the phone, he'd lose his focus. Her recovery took years of physical therapy and surgeries. Lots of setbacks. But at some point she was no longer satisfied with just sending her son letters and gifts on his birthday and never hearing back. With a cane and back brace she marched into the school and demanded to see her child."

"Did she have any concern at that point about abuse?"

"I'm not sure," Lincoln explained. "She'd given birth to my father by then, and she wanted her family back together. I don't know who Simon's father was; my grandmother never spoke about him, but I got the impression when she was injured he took off. My father knew his dad for a few years before he was killed in a traffic accident. He was a truck driver."

"Your grandmother experienced a lot of trauma in her life," Shayna sympathized.

"None was worse than what HIBS did to her. They deceived her, treated her like she was a fool."

"What do you believe happened to your uncle?" Shayna asked, scanning his features.

"There are whispers," Lincoln said quietly. "Very few people will speak about what happened at the school. Forget going on record; it's taboo for people who attended the school. My grandmother tried to find fellow students who might have known

Simon, but none would say much. Most advised her to stop pursuing it. But at her funeral a few people pulled me aside and told me a relative of theirs had also gone to HIBS and had been badly abused. They'd share bits and pieces of the story. They'd talk about how the kids were put in solitary confinement for days. The beatings were far more than just punishment; they were torture. I listened and was so angry they'd waited until my grandmother was dead to share the information. Then I realized why they had. It was one thing for her to believe my uncle had died and the school had been purposefully deceitful to her. If she knew what he had experienced all those years, I think it would have put her over the edge."

"Did anyone you spoke to know what happened to Simon specifically?" Shayna asked, trying to direct him back to the original question. She knew he didn't have the answer, but his speculation would come from a very raw place, and it was important to the story.

"No one did," Lincoln said, staring intently at the fire. "Are you warm enough?" he asked, catching the little shiver that rolled up her back.

"I'm fine. I think it's more the location than the temperature. I just keep thinking about what these kids went through. How long they've been here alone. There is one more thing. The tip I got about your uncle came from my uncle. He told me he thought he remembered that Simon got in trouble for having beads from the reservation and singing a song that wasn't in English. That was against the rules. He said Simon was healthy one day and being buried the next."

"Singing a song?" Lincoln asked, looking like he might be sick. "So it wasn't an accident? It was probably punishment."

"He couldn't say for sure. I intend to follow up with him again, but I'll be honest, he's been reluctant. He hasn't been in my life for many years, and I tracked him down to interrogate him about something he doesn't want to talk about."

"I didn't think I would ever meet anyone who cared about this the way I do. I thought Simon was the only one who didn't make it out of the school alive. I never imagined there was something like this." He gestured toward the graves and closed his eyes. "I'm really glad you called me."

"Me too," she admitted. "I have good friends who are helping me, but I'm not sure anyone is looking for exactly what we are."

"What would you call it? What are we looking for, justice?" he asked, his eyes now fixed on her face.

She matched his intense stare, and it took all the fire in her heart to muster a reply. "Revenge," she offered simply. "I want them to fall."

The familiar whistle echoed through the trees, and Shayna knew her brother was making his way back. She licked her lips and gave him the signal in return.

"He's going to want you to leave when he comes back?" Lincoln asked, sounding disappointed.

"Yeah," Shayna sighed. "I have to stay on the reservation as much as possible right now. There are people looking for me."

"People?" Lincoln furrowed his brows with concern.

"Cops," she admitted, still in disbelief that she'd gone from an honor student to a wanted criminal. If her mother knew, it would break her heart.

"Shayna," Tao said, the canteens under his arm as he tried to catch his breath. He'd clearly run back from the car, and she wondered what would have him so spooked.

"It's Mom," he breathed out. "They're taking her to the hospital. Some kind of complication."

Shayna sprang to her feet so fast she nearly toppled into the fire. Lincoln shot out an arm to catch her as he stood. "I'm sorry," she said, her nails digging into his forearm as she tried to keep herself rooted. Her grip on Lincoln was more than to steady her feet. A tornado of fear swirled around her, trying to suck her into the worst case scenario.

"It'll be all right," Lincoln said, having no way of knowing that.

"We have to go," Tao said, pulling Shayna in the direction of their car.

"If I'd have stayed out of this," Shayna said as they barreled through the brush tugging on them, "she'd in the right place, getting the best treatment."

"No," Tao said, not slowing down. "If they weren't monsters willing to gamble with people's lives to protect themselves from the truth, we wouldn't be in this position. We're going to expose them and get her help."

"What if it's too late?" Shayna gulped, feeling the urge to slow down, just as Tao sped up.

"Then I will make them all pay in ways they never imagined."

CHAPTER 21

Cancer was a vacuum. It hooked itself up to someone and sucked their life away. Her mother had worked double shifts, manual labor, impossible tasks. She was strong in the way only a single mother could be. Yet here in a hospital bed, all wires and colorless blankets, she was frail. Unrecognizable.

"I talked to Aunty in the lobby," Tao whispered as he came back into his mother's room. "She has to go to work so she can't stay."

"It's good she could get her here so quickly," Shayna said, her eyes still stinging with tears. A knock on the door sent her jumping.

"Sorry about that," the doctor apologized as he extended a hand and introduced himself. "My name is Dr. Z. I have one of those last names no one can pronounce." He cracked a smile, and Shayna felt his warmth fill the room. "I'm not your mother's doctor," he explained. "I'm having trouble finding her treatment history. Some is linked to our system, but there must be more I'm missing. Who is her oncologist?"

"It's a long story," Shayna sniffled, too tired to care about looking weak. "She was diagnosed five months ago by a clinic on our reservation. They helped transition her care to this hospital where she qualified for a clinical trial."

"I do see the trial information here. It seems like a good fit. Did she not tolerate the dose well? It's a fairly new drug, but its potential for someone with your mother's diagnosis is promising."

Shayna and Tao locked eyes, and she knew he was begging her not to say anything. It wasn't strategic. It wasn't calculated. But Dr. Z's mocha skin and thick-framed glasses were lulling her into believing he might be able to help.

"She was kicked out of it," Shayna explained. "She's now getting treatment at a clinic on the reservation my aunt lives on. They are not equipped to help her, as you can see." She gestured to her mother, who was forcing labored breaths in and out.

"She was kicked out of the clinical trial?" Dr. Z asked, looking at her chart and trying to find answers. "Did she fail to meet some criteria? Did she stop showing up?"

"I brought her here every week," Shayna explained. "She never missed anything. She followed every direction."

"That's odd," Dr. Z went on. "So you have no idea why she was removed from the trial?"

"We received a letter in the mail," Shayna said, wiping the tears from her cheeks. "Just some impersonal paragraph about how she was no longer a participant in the clinical trial and to please find alternative options for her health care needs."

"A letter?" Dr. Z replied, and Shayna saw him slipping into skepticism. "I can't imagine the doctor treating her would not provide a clear reason for why she would be dropped from the trial. Things do happen from time to time that disqualify candidates from clinical trials, but it is usually put through a small panel associated with the trial. I don't see any notes on file about their ruling."

"There wasn't one," Tao said flatly as he pulled the chair over to his mother's side and held her hand. "People like us are pretty easy to cast aside. Being poor and Indian."

"I . . . uh, I'm sure that . . ." Dr. Z stuttered. "There has to be more to the story than that. I can assure you I will work to find more information for you. But that's only part of the equation. We need to get your mother's current needs assessed. Can you help me with contact information?"

"I can," Shayna assured him. "When you find out why my mother was dropped, can you promise me you'll help us?"

"I can't promise she'll be added back to the trial. Not without knowing why they made the decision in the first place. But what I can guarantee you is, while your mother is in my care she will have every resource available to us. I don't care how much money you have or what your heritage is."

"Dr. Z," Shayna said in a low voice. "I believe they dropped her from the trial in order to put pressure on me about something. I can't share the details with you, but if you start looking into this and things don't add up, please keep what I said in mind. The decision was personal and made with malice. I don't expect you to believe me, because I'm offering you very little proof."

Dr. Z looked intently at Shayna and pursed his lips, looking reluctant to commit to anything he couldn't follow through with. "I'll try to get you an answer. In the meantime your mother needs to be hydrated and thoroughly checked. I'm getting on my shift now, so you can rest assured from now until morning, I have her covered."

"I'm going to stay," Tao asserted. "Shayna, I think it's best for you to go home. Send over the contact information for the clinic Mom has been going to."

Two nurses entered the room, and Shayna leaned down to kiss her mom goodbye. "Keep me posted," she said as she squeezed Tao's shoulder. "I'll send Frankie down to be here, too."

"Thanks," he said, "Only if she wants to."

"I think it would take wild horses to keep her from—" Shayna's words were cut short as Frankie skid into the room.

"Sorry I'm just getting here," she apologized. "For some reason they didn't believe I'm family. I think it's the freckles."

Shayna silently hugged her best friend, gave her a little nudge toward Tao, and headed for the door. All she wanted was to curl up in bed next to her mother and cry until her eyes ran dry. But she'd stopped being just a daughter. Shayna was a solider now, and the only way to win was to fight. She pushed the button anxiously on the elevator and wished it could teleport her to her house.

A far-off noise penetrated the edges of her mind, and she realized her phone was ringing. "Hello?" she asked, steading her voice as much as possible.

"Hey Shayna, it's Bobby," he said with excitement. "Guess what? I found the nurse. I'm texting her last known address. It's about an hour from the reservation. I couldn't find a phone number though. You'll have to go in cold."

"No problem," Shayna said, blinking herself back to reality. "Send it over."

"What's the matter?" Bobby asked, his tone shifting from excited optimist to worried cop who could tell something was up.

"My mother is back in the hospital. I think she'll be all right. She's dehydrated, I think. Some complications from her meds. The clinic can't provide enough bags of saline while they administer the chemo. They have limited resources."

"I'm sorry," Bobby apologized. "You should be with her now. Forget the other stuff."

"The other stuff," Shayna corrected, "will be what gets her back on the clinical trial. It's the only way I can really help her. I'm so grateful for the information. Hopefully, we can finally do something."

"Keep us posted on your mom," Bobby said, all the air

deflated now from him. "We'll be pulling for her. And stay safe. Take Piper with you when you go see the nurse."

"I will," Shayna promised. "She's been great. You are so lucky to have her."

"I know," Bobby agreed. "Just don't tell her I said that. We prefer to make fun of each other rather than shower compliments. It's our thing."

"I get that," Shayna said, managing a smile. "You guys are amazing. I'd be lost without the help."

"Be safe," he reminded her again.

They said their goodbyes as Shayna stepped outside the hospital into the night air. The automatic door closed behind her and trapped all the busy hospital noise inside. It would be a long sleepless night of worry. If she couldn't rest, she figured she might as well fill the time with something distracting.

She sent a quick text to Piper and switched her phone to silent. She'd check it often enough to know if there were any updates on her mother, but otherwise she'd close out the rest of the world. Well, all but one person.

CHAPTER 22

She hoped the whistle would be enough to warn Lincoln she was coming back. She could smell the occasional scent of smoke as she grew closer, and finally he replied with a whistle.

"You're back?" he asked, rolling his sleeping bag out for her to sit on. "Is your mom all right?"

"I don't know," she shrugged, refusing to cry. "She's at the hospital, and the doctor seemed to be nice. I just couldn't stay there. They're actively looking for me, and if they know she's been admitted, they'll assume I'm with her."

"So you'll hide out here by their property?" Lincoln asked, with a raised brow. "Isn't that what your brother was worried about?"

"Well now he has bigger things to worry about," Shayna snapped back as she sank onto the sleeping bag. "I have an address for the nurse who used to work at the school. I'm going there first thing in the morning. If anyone can tell us what happened to your uncle, I bet it would be her."

"You're just going to go knock on her door?" Lincoln asked, looking doubtful.

"Yes. The same way I just dialed your number and knocked

on the other doors to get people on record. If I warn her, it gives her time to decide she doesn't want to talk to me."

"I want to talk to your uncle," Lincoln said as though the idea had been brewing in his mind since they'd talked earlier. "Can you make that happen?"

"I don't know," Shayna admitted. "We didn't leave things well. He's very rattled. I don't want to hurt him or make him do anything he doesn't want to. He suffered there, too. Who am I to force him to relive that?"

"Would he come here tonight?" Lincoln asked. "If you called him and told him where you were and what was happening, wouldn't he be worried enough to come?"

"Are you asking if I'll trick him into coming here? Will I manipulate him and his emotions to get what I want?"

"Yes," Lincoln said, looking mildly uncomfortable by the truth.

"Let me see if he answers my text first," she said, firing off a message to him and then tucking her phone away before she could see if Piper was nagging her to come home.

"Why did you come back here?" Lincoln asked, putting a few small pieces of timber over the flames to keep it going.

Shayna thought on it, not entirely sure of the answer herself. "I can go if I'm intruding," she offered. "I know this is kind of sacred ground to you."

"I'm glad you came back," Lincoln admitted. "I see something when I look at you. Something I like."

She laughed nervously as she pulled her hair off her face and tucked it back. "You're pretty blunt."

"I mean something I understand. It's like I've been a tourist in a foreign land where everyone speaks a foreign language and navigates life easily. I was just plopped here and am fumbling. And then you came by and said all the things I've been feeling for most of my life. That thing I see in you I like, I'm pretty sure it's just anger. But that's a language I can understand."

"Yeah," Shayna agreed, nodding her head as she reached for a bag of chips. "Anger sounds right."

"Have you always lived on reservation?" Lincoln asked, but judging by his look, he seemed to know the answer to that already. "You've traveled? Seen the world?"

"Not the world." She chuckled. "Some states. Nothing all that exotic, but I went to a school off reservation and had a lot of opportunities. It was nothing like this school. Or at least I didn't think so."

"What do you mean?"

"I always felt I was making all the choices in my life, but now when I look back, they really pushed me hard onto the path I took. I had a spark of potential, and they insisted I grow it into a bigger flame. That meant being more like them and less like me. Before I knew it, I was the Indian girl breaking records and meeting their quota for minorities. I'm not saying it didn't feel good. I loved the recognition and the praise. The spotlight on me during a competition was an adrenaline rush. But I'm not sure I understood what I had to trade in order to achieve what they wanted for me at that young age. All I accomplished was pretending to be like everyone else some days and allowing myself to be the token brown person other days."

"You think you're looking for someone to blame for this?" Lincoln asked, folding his hands and tucking them under his chin.

"Yes," she acknowledged. "And I get how that could be unhealthy. But I actually believe they are to blame. Not only for my father drinking himself to death, but for far more. No one should be given that level of power on the backs of innocent people."

"Close your eyes," Lincoln said, reaching over and grabbing her hand. Her first response was to pull away, but she fought that.

His hand was warm, and his grip wasn't forced or demanding. "Trust me," he pleaded.

She blew out a nervous breath and closed her eyes.

"The spirits are with us here," he began. "Peace is within reach for them if we, well, if you, can help them. If it's revenge in your heart, let it grow big enough to overtake them. I don't think it matters why you're doing it. Just do it." They opened their eyes, but he continued to hold her hand gently.

"What if I fail? What if I pull off all of this and it's still not enough? Former students claiming they suffered and witnessed corporal punishment and downright abuse. A lot full of unmarked graves. Rumors of murder. Documentation from their own records that support the claims. We can show they were behind my mother losing critical medical care and they were the reason my scholarships were revoked. Maybe, if I'm lucky, a former staff member who's willing to break her silence about what she witnessed there and was subsequently fired for speaking up. We package that up. We expose it to the world, and we find out, just like we have so many times before, the world doesn't care. Or they don't care enough to actually do anything about it."

"I hope I haven't given you the impression I'm profound or even mildly articulate. I don't know what you should do if you fail. Just don't fail."

The corners of her mouth lifted into a smile she had no control over. "You're right, not very profound."

He chuckled and squeezed her hand. "I'm sorry I couldn't be of more help. Is there anything else I can do? I'll get the tapes from my grandmother. I've already called a friend to have her dig them out and take them to you."

"Your girlfriend?" Shayna asked, feeling instantly like an idiot. "Or I mean—"

"Just a friend I've known since kindergarten. She's not my

girlfriend. She's actually another girl's girlfriend, which is about as far from being mine as you can get."

They were both laughing now as a coyote howled far in the distance. "I don't know why I asked you that; I'm sorry."

"Maybe you were thinking of your own boyfriend. What's he's like?"

"I don't have one," she dismissed quickly. Too quickly to be anything besides weird. "I mean I have had one. But I don't have one now."

"Do you need a drink or something?" he asked, narrowing his eyes at her. "You seem a little—" Before he could finish his offer she was leaning in and pressing her lips to his. Reckless . . . Impractical . . . Then as his lips parted and over took hers, the words melted away. Recklessly magical . . . Impractically perfect . . . Exactly what she needed.

Her phone vibrated in her pocket as their lips parted and eyes darted away. She yanked it out and read the screen with some relief. "It's my uncle. He said he'd be willing to talk some time. Should I have him come here?"

"I thought so five minutes ago," Lincoln admitted as he pushed his hair back and grinned. "Now I'm not sure what the hell I'm thinking anymore."

Her phone chimed again. "Never mind. He says he left town for a while. He needed to clear his head. He'll think about it for when he's back."

Lincoln didn't reply. He examined her face the way someone would search for a particular puzzle piece in a giant pile. Another text chimed on her phone, and she was about to toss it into the brush. But it was her brother.

Tao: I know you went back there. I saw how you were looking at him. Don't make this messier than it already is.

Shayna: Butt out. It's not like that. How's Mom?

Tao: More tests coming. She's awake now. I told her you'd see her soon. That you were at school.

Shayna: You've always been a better liar.

Tao: Obviously because I can see right through what you're doing right now. Go home.

Shayna: Keep me posted on Mom. We're going to see the HIBS nurse in the a.m.

She tapped the screen to close the message and put the phone away. "My mother is awake now. She still needs lots of tests."

Lincoln was standing now, adjusting the fire and listening intently to the noises of the night around them. "I'll walk you back to your car. You shouldn't be going back and forth alone. It's too dark."

"I agree," she, said, lying down on the sleeping bag and closing her eyes. "Much safer at sunrise."

"You can't stay here all night," he protested, looking at her like she was mad. "Your brother doesn't seem like a dude I really want to deal with. I have enough to deal with in my life, I don't need your big brother calling me out for a fist fight to protect your honor."

"He's my younger brother," Shayna corrected, but Lincoln didn't look deterred by the detail.

"It's a bad idea," he objected, but she could already tell by the softness of his voice he was giving in.

"I'm not suggesting anything beyond that kiss should happen tonight, if you're so worried about defending my honor. I prefer to keep it intact myself. I just want to crash here tonight, under the stars the way I used to. I want to have a night where I'm the native descendant who knows her roots and embraces the earth as her blanket and the moon as her nightlight. I don't want to be the college girl who happens to be interesting because she's an Indian."

"Get that tape recorder out," Lincoln said, pointing at her bag.

"I'm going on record as protesting this. But if you're giving me no other choice, I'll have to find a way to put up with you."

"Trust me, that's no easy task. Just ask around."

He pulled his sweatshirt over his head and tossed it to her. "I don't know how long it's been since dirt has been your bed and the sky your nightlight or whatever, but it'll be cold. Help me tie this hammock. You can sleep in that. You don't want to be on the ground. Scorpions."

"You don't have to accommodate me. I just want to be here." She stood and cut the distance between them to a few inches. "I just want to be somewhere that feels real. This place feels as close to the truth as I can get. Tomorrow morning, I start again. My mother is still sick. I'll go ambush an unsuspecting older woman with a barrage of questions she'll be unlikely to want to answer. It's all waiting for me out there." She pointed through the tree line back toward where her car was parked. She slipped his sweatshirt over her head and drew in a deep breath. His earthy musk enveloped her, as tangible as the warmth of the cotton.

He reached in his pocket and pulled out his cell phone. Tapping at the screen, he cued up a song and extended his hand to her. "Do you dance?" he asked as the singer's sultry voice filled the space between them.

"I do tonight," she replied, falling into his arms and resting her head on his chest. With far more skill than she gave him credit, Lincoln led her through the dance, his hand firmly on the small of her back.

The thudding of his heart filled her ear and drowned out all other thoughts. The songs bled together. The minutes melted away.

"You good?" he whispered into her hair.

"This is ridiculous," she sighed. "Ridiculous and perfect."

CHAPTER 23

Shayna had bypassed this part of her youth. She'd never stayed out all night and had to ready herself for the wrath that waited back home. She was a rule follower. A people pleaser. There was no way to know how Piper was going to reprimand her, but she imaged the worst.

Not having a lot of practice at disappointing people, she wasn't sure if she should go in, spouting her explanation before the door even opened. Or maybe drop to her knees and beg forgiveness. She didn't have time for either. Piper stepped outside, dressed and ready to go with two coffees in her hand.

"I have a clean shirt, a brush, and some makeup in my bag. Let's get on the road." She handed one coffee to Shayna and gestured for the car keys. Shayna handed them over and waited for something more dramatic to happen. But it didn't. Piper got in the driver seat and fired up the engine. When Shayna didn't move Piper beeped the horn, sending her jumping.

Finally she shot into motion and got into the passenger seat. There was still a chance the yelling would start once she was completely stuck in the locked car, speeding down the road. But they made it a few miles and still nothing.

"Why aren't you yelling at me?" Shayna finally asked, unable to deal with the lack of reaction from Piper.

"Do you want me to yell at you?" Piper asked, giving her an odd look. "Or do you want to agree that you're an adult, and you can decide where you spend the night."

"But I was in the woods with a stranger near the property of the people who are trying to arrest me." When she said it all out loud Shayna couldn't believe she was talking about herself. It was not at all like her to string that many stupid things together. "I can't believe I did that. It was dangerous. Reckless. I was jeopardizing everything we're doing. No," Shayna said, wagging her finger animatedly. "You know what it was? Selfish. It was completely selfish of me. I just wanted to disappear, fade out for a night. But it's sheer luck this didn't bite us in the ass. Stupid."

Piper laughed and covered her mouth.

"What's so funny?" Shayna asked, sounding like a pouty toddler.

"Sorry," Piper said, half-heartedly trying to stifle her laugh. "You're like one of those pianos you put a quarter in, and you play yourself. I figured if I waited long enough you'd figure out how dumb that was. I've known you long enough, kid. No one is harder on Shayna than Shayna. Now get yourself cleaned up. You have leaves in your hair."

Shayna frantically stroked her long hair and pulled a few stray pieces of nature out. "You know, I didn't—I mean he and I didn't."

"You heard me, kid, I've known you long enough. I'm actually glad you ran away for a little while. With everything going on, and your mom being admitted, you'd explode if you didn't take a break. Nicholas didn't ask where you were, and I didn't tell him. I'm assuming he figured you were at the hospital, and I didn't correct him."

"Oh gosh," she groaned, covering her face in shame.

"Nicholas. I have no idea what I'm doing there. Am I leading him on? Am I using him?"

"I am," Piper said evenly. "He had a taxi come for him this morning, and he's off to do a bunch of prep work I need for getting those documents. I'm going once we're done with the nurse. What's her name again?"

"Cybil Willis. She never married. She never moved. I have no clue what we're walking into."

"We won't be walking into anything with you looking like that," Piper said, reaching over and flipping the mirror down. "Brush."

CHAPTER 24

The house looked as though it had been pulled from the pages of a magazine. A quaint cottage on a quiet cul-de-sac, completely unassuming. Charm oozed from the lemon shutters and flower boxes stuffed full of colorful blooms.

"Forget all this stuff," Piper said, leaning to get a better look at the house as they approached. "Let's see if she'll let us move in."

"You're not nervous?" Shayna asked, watching the little bounce in Piper's step and her casual stance.

"This is the good part," Piper said, trying to reassure her. "The waiting and the planning. That's the torture in my book. Finally getting to knock on the door and see if you get what you came for. There's nothing to be nervous about."

The porch boards creaked under their feet as Piper lifted the metal knocker and gently banged it down two times. It felt like only a heartbeat before a tiny woman with platinum blonde hair found only in a bottle answered. She wore a knit vest over a long-sleeved silk blouse with polyester pants. The chain that held her glasses dangling around her neck had little beads with cats printed on them.

"Hello, girls," she sang out in such a friendly way it felt as though she'd been expecting them. "What a lovely surprise."

"Hi," Shayna said, fumbling for words, taken aback by the woman's warmth. "Are you Cybil Willis?"

"I am indeed," Cybil said, pulling her glass on. "And who are you lovely little things?"

"My name is Piper; this is Shayna. We have something we want to talk with you about, but it's of a sensitive nature. We don't want to make you uncomfortable, so please let us know if you mind us chatting with you."

"I love a good chat," Cybil said, swinging her door open wider and gesturing for them to come in. "Are you hungry?"

"Ah," Shayna hesitated at the doorstep but Piper waltzed right in.

"We had a long drive in from the Tewapi reservation, so we didn't have a chance to eat. We'd love a little something if it's not too much trouble."

"It's not at all," Cybil said, her voice rising in excitement.

"Are you sure you want to feed us and stuff?" Shayna asked, only a couple feet in to the cottage now. "You don't know why we're here."

"Do you want a little tea or coffee too?" Cybil asked, dismissing Shayna's concern. "Close that door up, dear, it's hot out there, and I have the fans running."

"Yes ma'am," Shayna finally said and closed the door. She took a quick inventory of the entryway and living room. All beach themed and bright colors. A seashell wallpaper border rimmed the room, and everything nautical was spread across all available spaces. Not a very common decor for a house in the desert. "You love the ocean?" Shayna asked as she joined Piper and Cybil in the kitchen. A store-bought coffee cake was sliced and water boiled in a kettle on the stove. Cybil was quick.

"I love the ocean," Cybil replied, exaggerating the words. "I collect all sorts of things from the sea."

"What's your favorite beach?" Piper asked, happily accepting the coffee cake with a smile.

"Well," Cybil replied, her face falling slightly for the first time since their arrival, "I've never actually been to the sea, but I've dreamed of it all my life."

"What's kept you from going?" Shayna asked, accepting the far too big slice of coffee cake balanced on a napkin.

"Life, girl. Life."

"I hear that," Piper laughed. "I have twins at home, a job, and my husband is a police officer. Life has a way of changing our plans."

"So ladies," Cybil said, sitting down at the old metal and vinyl table with them, "what church are you with? I'll be honest, I'm not really looking for a new religion, but I do like to keep myself informed. Last month I had a group of young people talking to me about a new kind of charity. So interesting."

"We're sorry if we weren't clear," Piper said, taking a nibble of her dry coffee cake. "Shayna and I aren't here for something like that. Shayna's father and uncle were students at the Hillder-staff Indian Boarding School." She paused, and to her credit Cybil didn't flinch a bit.

"I worked there for a time," she replied as though she were commenting on a movie she'd seen.

"We know that," Shayna chimed in. "That's why we're here. I don't want to put you on the spot, but the rumor was you were fired because you weren't willing to participate in or cover up the abuse taking place there."

"No," Cybil cut in, waving her finger, "the rumor was I was having an affair with a staff member there and got pregnant. What you said was the truth. The other part was pure slander to scare me off. I'm sad to say, it was a different time back then, and it worked. It sent me running for the hills.

"So you witnessed abuse at the school?" Shayna pressed.

"First hand," Cybil said, nodding seriously. "But it didn't start that way. Just like most of the staff, I was shielded from it for a long time. They wanted to know you were loyal to them before they'd pull that curtain back and show you the horrors."

"Why haven't you spoken up about this before today?" Shayna asked, her heart racing with anxiety.

"I've been waiting for you," Cybil replied simply. "Or someone like you who wanted to hear the story. Dealing with people like those at HIBS is sort of like being in a warzone. I've been pinned down all these years, and I knew one voice wouldn't be enough. I didn't have the trust of the indigenous community. No one would speak to me or with me about any of it. There were plenty of times at the school you'd see policemen collecting money in exchange for what I understood to be cover-ups. When I left the school, I was a broken woman. I didn't believe anyone could be trusted anymore. I regret my silence, but I always believed there would be a day when someone would come knocking, and I wouldn't be pinned down or alone anymore."

"Did they make you sign any contracts or paperwork saying you wouldn't discuss what you saw there?" Piper gestured for Shayna to start recording and Cybil nodded her agreement.

"They tried," she explained. "They came around about five or so years after I was fired, and they pressured me to sign something along those lines. They offered money. They offered to pay off my mortgage. I told them I wasn't interested. The threats started, but I'd been so ruined by them already, it was like they couldn't sink any lower to hurt me. Every now and then over the next few years I'd get a phone call from their lawyer, and I'd tell them the same thing. Leave me in peace."

"People are talking now, Cybil," Shayna assured her. "There

are students coming forward. We even found the grave site with the bodies."

"Oh my," she gasped, covering her mouth with her hands. "I begged them to give those boys a proper burial. I grew up near a reservation as a child. I knew the customs were special and HIBS was stomping all over them."

"I have a difficult question for you, Cybil," Shayna said directly. "Did you witness the murder or some kind of abuse that resulted in death of any child at HIBS?"

"No," Cybil replied clearly for the tape recorder. "At first they brought me the boys who were sick. Other nurses worked on other injuries and such. Then after about a year, they started bringing the boys who had been paddled. Then the ones who were whipped. The injuries coming in my door got worse and worse, and there was always some story to accompany it. Some reason the boy was beaten as badly as he was. Or that he fell or was in a fight with an older boy."

"Do you remember incidences of death? You must have had boys who were there one day and gone the next. Or here," Shayna said, pulling out the original list of names that started all of this. "These children were all listed as deceased. Here are their dates of death. Do any stand out to you?"

She scanned the list quickly and put a finger to her chin as she thought. "Wait, I was told these boys were adopted by families on the reservation. They were orphans, and I was happy for them. The youngest one was so sweet. It happened over a few months, if I remember right."

"So you were working in the medical ward at the time, servicing all the students, and you didn't know these three boys died? They weren't ill or in your care at all?"

"They weren't," she said confidently. The older one here would come in every now and then for some ice packs on the welts he'd get from a whipping."

"What eventually happened that ended your career there?" Piper asked.

"There were two boys who had taken some food from the cafeteria after they had already finished their meals. I was there helping out, and I saw the moment they were caught. One of the worst men there, his name was Oxford, caught them and yanked them right outside. I followed them because I wanted to know what was going on. I was tired of stitching up broken skin and treating lash marks. He took them out back to a spot I hadn't been in. I knew what happened in there, and I didn't want to see it. I didn't like to see the boys hurt, but I had been told these were dangerous children in need of civilizing and rehabilitation. These men said they were doing the work, the very hard work, to save these boy's lives in the long run. That day I wanted to see it for myself. I tucked myself in the corner of that little building, and I watched maybe sixty seconds of that beating before I jumped in and demanded they stop. I walked through there and found boys no older than nine being starved and in solitary confinement. I will tell you I blew through that place like a run-away train, and no one could stop me. I had every boy released and demanded I speak with the Hillderstaff family immediately. The boys were fed, washed up, and left in my office to be checked out."

"I bet they were grateful you helped them."

"I ran away and failed them miserably. Gregory Hillderstaff arrived in less than twenty minutes, and he told me I was no longer employed. I won't take credit where none is due. There was such suffering there, and yes, that was the first time I saw it with my own eyes. I had known for some time things weren't right. I was a coward."

Piper reached a hand out and touched her arm gently. "Now is the time to do something. You aren't a single voice anymore. You can help validate some of the stories we're hearing. Being on staff gives you a whole different perspective and an additional layer of credibility."

"I'm ready for that," Cybil said. "I mean they aren't going to go around now and tell people I'm pregnant."

The three women chuckled at the idea, and Cybil continued to recount all she could about her time at the school and the children listed as deceased.

"Do you remember Simon Coldwater?" Shayna asked hopefully. "He arrived there when he was ten and stayed until he was fourteen."

"No, he didn't," Cybil said, her eyes flashing with memories. "He was only there a year, maybe a year and a half. I remember looking for him one day in the lunch line, and he was gone. When I inquired no one was sure where he was. Other students told me he'd gotten in trouble for having some necklace or beads or something. I went to see a few staff members who were primarily responsible for punishment, and they told me he'd run away. This was years before I took my head out of the sand and found out what was really going on."

"Do you believe Simon Coldwater ran away?" Shayna asked.

"There is no way for me to know," Cybil said apologetically. "I just know he was not at the school for nearly five years, it was just over one year. To the best of my knowledge, he was never reported missing, even though he was only ten years old."

To Cybil's credit her stamina far exceeded Frankie's expectations. The conversation went on for nearly two hours, and her candidness never faded. Cybil admitted where she failed the kids and grew angry when she remembered certain parts. When the coffee cake was gone and the tea was empty, Piper stood and clasped her hands together gratefully.

"Cybil, you have done an amazing service today. You're joining a small but mighty group of people, and we're getting this story distributed to the world."

"They won't like that," Cybil said, for the first time in this entire process looking nervous. "Maybe it's finally time I see that beach. There's nothing left around here for me to wait for, now that you've come."

Shayna rose, reluctant to turn off the tape recorder since Cybil seemed so engaged. "Are you saying the reason you never traveled or went to the beach you seem to love so much is because you were worried you'd miss the arrival of someone looking for answers about HIBS?"

"You took longer than I thought. I'll admit that," she chuckled a bit as they headed toward the door and lingered.

"Safe travels then," Piper said, pulling Cybil in for a hug. "You were great today."

"You girls be safe. There is almost nothing they'll stop at to keep the past buried. If you need more than just that statement you've recorded, I'll leave you my contact information.

The goodbye dragged on a few more minutes, the conversations dying down and then suddenly ramping back up with more friendly chatter. When they finally went to the car, Shayna felt like she might be sick.

"We may need to pull over on the way home," she said, holding her stomach. "I don't know why, but I'm shaky and queasy."

"It could be the coffee cake," Piper suggested. "But more likely it's the adrenaline winding down and leaving you feeling shot. That's a good thing. It means we're getting closer."

Shayna's phone began to buzz, and she felt her nausea rise even higher when she saw it was the hospital calling.

"Shayna, it's Dr. Z. Is now a good time for us to talk?" His voice was low and guarded, and Shayna worried it was terrible news.

"Yes," she replied stiffly.

"I did some digging into the clinical trial, and it turns out not one member of the review board associated with the trial knew anything about your mother's case. They had assumed her lack of participation in the trial was her choice."

"It wasn't," Shayna cut back quickly.

"I know that. Your brother provided me with a copy of the letter you received. None of the board members were familiar with that either and insisted policy for removing someone from a clinical trial included face-to-face consultation. Never a letter. After meeting with your mom and looking at the few notes that remain here, I find her to be of sound mind and meeting the criteria set forth for the trial."

"So she can start again with the new medicine?"

Dr. Z. hesitated, dropping his voice down even lower. "If she were my mother I would not continue having her treated at this hospital. A full investigation will need to be launched into who tampered with her records and who sent this letter. I'd seek treatment elsewhere as soon as possible. There are seven other hospitals performing this trial. Countless others testing the medicine in a less structured way."

"We can't afford to find another hospital. When we lost our opportunity there, she had to seek treatment at the reservation clinic."

"She cannot continue being treated there," Dr. Z. said firmly. "I spoke with them this morning. They are not equipped to care for her unique medical needs. Your brother told me you have some people in North Carolina. There are three teaching hospitals there that are currently running this study. Would your friends be willing to help support your mother while she underwent treatment there?"

"Uh, I mean I could ask them," Shayna stuttered. "But how would I get her there? She's in no condition to fly or take the train."

"I could set up a medical transport, but it would have to be today. In trying to find the answers, I've had to involve more people than I would have liked, and I don't know how long it will stay quiet. If this is a personal vendetta, and it runs as high as you say it does, we need to move fast."

"I'll have to ask my friends if they're willing to help my mother in North Carolina. I can get back to you in—"

Piper leaned over and spoke into the phone. "Send her as soon as you can. We're happy to support her in North Carolina. Let us know where to be and when."

"So that's it then," Dr. Z said anxiously. "I'm going to move forward. Your brother is going to travel with her. Once she's safely settled and receiving the treatment she needs, I'll ensure this investigation does not get sidelined. I want answers."

"Why did you do all this?" Shayna asked, feeling weepy at the idea her mother might actually have the help she needs now.

"I'm ashamed to say when you left, what ran through my mind about why your mother wasn't a part of the trial anymore was what you could have done to lose the opportunity. I assumed it was some kind of failure on her part, and that you were looking for someone to blame. Never for a minute did I think your mother's health care was being used as some kind of leverage to get what they want from you. Once I started to see you were telling the truth, I knew I owed you not only an apology but a solution. Now I'm going to get to work on this. Expect your brother to keep you posted."

"Thank you, Dr. Z," Shayna said as he hung up the phone.

"My mom is going to Edenville," Shayna said in disbelief.

Piper grinned widely. "She'll be in great hands there, you know that. I don't think you could have a better outcome for her than that."

"It's so much to ask. I don't know when I'll be able to join her and help out," Shayna said, the reality of her situation finally setting in. "It's too much."

"Stop," Piper said, waving her worry away. "If there is anything I know for sure, it's that when Betty gets this phone call she'll nearly collapse with excitement, knowing she can help your mother in a more tangible way than just wishing her well."

"I can't believe this is happening," she said, finally allowing a little smile to form on her face. "She's going to Edenville. She's going to be safe."

CHAPTER 25

"You're heading to the bunker with Nicholas then?" Shayna asked as they pulled in the driveway and saw him walking around the property anxiously.

"Yes," Piper replied, eying him curiously. "You're staying here. I need you to start editing the tape you have and reaching out to the contact Nicholas had for us."

"How's your mom?" Nicholas asked nervously, biting at his thumbnail. "Did you get to talk to Cybil this morning? I need an update."

Shayna smiled at his concern and filled him in on everything. "Now it's up to you guys to get some hard documented evidence from their files. I'm certain you'll find something that backs up the stories we heard. I'm working on prepping the tapes and the information we already have. I'm ready for you to put me in contact with Kevin Stone."

"Already?" Nicholas asked, a wash of renewed worry filling his face. "I mean it's hardly print ready at this point."

"I know," Shayna said, feeling suddenly self-conscious. "But I think he'll have everything he needs to at least get started. We need to know he's interested."

Nicholas clicked through his phone and sent a message that was almost instantly replied to. "I'll set a meeting for the two of you today. Lunch? I'll text you an address."

"Perfect," she beamed. "I can't thank you enough for all the help. Anything you get out of the bunker today will be the nail in the coffin."

"For my family," he said, reminding her the casualties he might suffer in all of this. "So then what happens?"

"What do you mean?" Shayna asked, furrowing her brows in confusion as they all came into the house. "We know what we want to happen. Kevin Stone picks up the story, and we go public. Maybe charges will be filed. Maybe people will be held accountable, but at the end of the day, at least the story will be out there. I want him to include that, legally, the document people signed for silence doesn't include everything they were led to believe. I bet once people see the story, more will come forward."

"I meant what do we do?" he asked in a hushed voice as Piper made her way to the kitchen. "This whole time you've been saying nothing could happen between us because we were too invested in this, too distracted. It'll be done soon, and then what happens between us?"

Shayna's thoughts went immediately to Lincoln. An impractical landing point for her brain right now, but the connection she felt with him in just a day far outweighed the one she had with Nicholas after all this time. In her mind, she had assumed it might blossom over time. Maybe when all this was behind them, she really could picture a future for herself. His phone chimed again and he huffed. "Your lunch is set up. I'm sending you the address. Listen, I'm putting my neck out for you today. I'm going to essentially rob my family to make a case against them. I really thought we were doing this for a reason, for us to maybe have something. Now it seems like that's not the case."

"I've been pretty clear on my reasons for doing this," Shayna countered. "I never implied that we'd have some happily ever after. I might be going to jail. My future is not exactly crystal clear right now."

"Haven't I proven to you I'm not afraid of a bumpy future? I've stuck around through all of this. I've put my own life on hold to help you. I'm not the one acting afraid to commit, no matter how uncertain it is." He crossed the living room and brushed his hand across her cheek. "I've known since the moment I first met you that I wanted to be with you. There hasn't been a single thing that's come up that's changed my mind. What else do I need to do to prove it to you? Because I'll tell you something, I'm not going in there today and breaking the law if there's no point to it."

"No point to it?" Shayna sputtered out. "You know as well as I do what's on the line. You know what they've been accused of. People deserve justice. They deserve the truth to be told. I thought that's why you were here."

"You know damn well I wanted to be with you," he said like a petulant child who'd been promised a reward and never received it. "No one is stupid enough to do all this and then get nothing back in return."

"So you assumed we'd finish this, and I'd just sleep with you? Is that the payment you're looking for? Maybe we should have drawn up a contract."

His voice grew sharper. "Maybe we should have so you wouldn't have used me and then ditched me the second you got what you wanted. Tell me the truth; will you get your documents and your meeting with Kevin Stone and then be done with me?"

"I like you, Nicholas. You're my friend. I never promised you more than that, and it isn't the reason you said you were here. If that's all you want from me, if that's the payment you thought you were going to get, forget all this. I'll do it on my own."

"You can't," Nicholas bit back. "Piper needs me there today, and I can easily cancel the lunch with Stone. You can't do this without me. You never could."

"What do you want from me?" Shayna hissed. "What's it going to take?"

"We leave," Nicholas said, sounding like he'd planned it all out long before this. "Forget the charges against you. Forget the fallout from this. You and I take my college money, and we get out of here. Far away. Some beach where no one can find us, and we have each other." He leaned down and tipped her chin up to steal a kiss. His tongue invaded her mouth, and she gave in as thoughts swirled in her mind. She was not guilt-free in this. She was not absolved of the fact that she could have been clearer with him about her feelings. Eventually she broke the kiss and leaned back.

"I can't commit to that," she apologized. "I'm not going to run away from this. I'm going to face the consequences and be here for my mother when she needs me." There was a chance if she didn't have a kiss so recent and so magical to compare it to, the adrenaline of the moment might have swept her up. She could have perhaps molded her feelings into something that resembled chemistry between them. But the night with Lincoln had set the bar too high. It had been a reminder of how being understood could connect you.

"We need to leave," Piper said, interrupting at the most perfectly imperfect moment. "Our window of time is small; it needs to be today."

"Sure," Nicholas said, looking like he was near tears. "Let's go."

"Nicholas," Shayna said, following them to the door, "we'll talk more about it tonight. We're in the home stretch, and emotions are running high. It'll be clearer later."

"Yeah, it will be."

CHAPTER 26

Kevin Stone never showed, and the pit in Shayna's stomach felt like the size of a canyon. The only good news she'd gotten was that Tao had his mother safely settled on the medical transport and everyone in Edenville would be waiting, ready to help. Frankie, torn between going with them or staying to help Shayna, needed a push from her friend. "Tao needs you more," Shayna had said, reminding her it wouldn't be good for any of them to be hanging around here when the story broke. She still had Piper and Nicholas, so she'd be fine. She hadn't told her best friend what had happened between them.

After waiting two hours for Stone to show up, Shayna paid her bill and stared at her phone, willing it to ring with news. Finally Piper called and Shayna fumbled to answer it quickly.

"How did it go?" she blurted out.

"Fine," Piper said, sounding anything but fine. "Nicholas and I had to go in different directions when things got a little dicey. He has all the documents, and I'm heading back to the house now. I'm sure he'll meet us there. How did things go with the reporter?"

"He never showed," Frankie said nervously. "That seems like

a bad sign, right?"

A cold sweat broke across her neck as a familiar voice rattled behind her. Sheriff Dobbins stood a foot or so back and cackled, "You had me running to the damn coast looking for you, and the whole time you were back here?"

"I have to go, Piper. There's a copy of everything at the house. Get it quickly." Shayna held her backpack over the drain in the sidewalk at her feet and listened as the water rushed by. There was run off from the restaurants power washing their awnings and stone. She slid her backpack off her shoulders, and in one move, kicked it down the drain. It was swept up in the rush of the water and gone a second later.

"What the hell was in there?" Dobbins asked frantically as he knelt by the drain just in time to see it vanish. "You're under arrest," he said, hopping to his feet and spinning her around quickly.

"Did Nicholas tell you where I was?" Shayna asked, holding her breath as he pinched her wrists with the metal cuffs. "The boy finally smartened up and stopped chasing your tail all over the country. I don't know what the hell you two were doing, but some powerful people want it stopped. And now it is."

"This was always bigger than me," Shayna corrected. "I knew I'd be arrested. That doesn't stop the truth from coming out. You're no different from the people they've been hiring to enforce their cruelty."

"Cruelty? You're the one who assaulted someone. You broke into a place you had no business being in. Don't play the victim now."

Shayna pursed her lips and listened to him read her rights loud enough to draw everyone's eyes her way. He tossed her into the back of his car, and she prayed Piper would get back to all of her work before Nicholas would. She'd scorned him, and he was going to strike back.

CHAPTER 27

The only thing on Shayna's mind was finding out if Piper had reached the house in time to get the extra copies of everything. So when a familiar faced passed right in front of her, she didn't light with recognition.

"Shayna?" Lincoln asked, grunting when the officer holding his cuffs tugged him backward. "I guess I can stop assuming you were the one who called the cops on me."

"Yeah," she said, blinking the emotion out of her eyes. "But it is my fault either way. I involved someone in this we couldn't trust, and he sold us out."

The officers escorting both of them had them sit on the bench and told them to wait for their names to be called.

"I had to literally throw all the work I'd done down the drain. I'm hoping Piper beat Nicholas back to the house to get the copies I made," Shayna whispered and fidgeted nervously.

"They got me for trespassing. Some blond kid and an old guy were there taking a bunch of pictures. Talking all about the story they were going to break."

"Oh my gosh," Shayna said, dropping her head down. "He's

not selling us out to his family so they can quiet us. He's stealing the story, so he can put his name on it."

"Then why are you smiling?" Nicholas asked, clearly worried she might have had a mental breakdown.

"Because nothing will make this story more compelling than having his name on it. It's one thing for some 'Indian girl' to talk about problems in her own culture's history. Everyone expects that. You put a rich white kid's face on it and have him turning against his own family. That story will go viral."

"We've been arrested," Lincoln said, clearly unable to see the bright side. "I'll be out soon enough. Trespassing isn't anything. But you fled. Your charges are more serious. Who knows what will happen to you?"

Piper stormed through the police station door and flung her arms around Shayna. "That little bastard took everything."

"It's all right. He's not trying to burying it; he's trying to expose it." Shayna laughed. "Kevin Stone didn't show up with me because he was meeting Nicholas instead. He's going to break this story."

"Oh," Piper said, thinking it over. "That's good. That's actually great."

"You guys are strange," Lincoln said, rolling his eyes. "I'm going to pummel this guy if I ever see him."

With impeccable timing, Nicholas walked through the door with three men trailing behind him. One was the reporter, Kevin Stone. "I want these two out of cuffs now," Nicholas ordered. Their lawyers are here, and they won't be saying another word to any of you."

"Our lawyers?" Shayna asked, wide-eyed.

"Yes," Nicholas said with his chin held high. "You're not going to spend a second more time here than it takes to fill out paperwork. I've already contacted the man pressing charges for assault, and he's agreed to drop them. Everything is under control."

"Listen you little—" Piper said, shooting to her feet.

"Piper don't," Shayna begged. "This is the best way for this to happen. Nicholas has it under control."

At that statement, Nicholas lit with pride. "There's more. I was very busy the last few hours. There's an anthropologist willing to work with me to excavate the gravesite and work to positively identify the bodies there. I'm expecting to hear from my grandfather any minute. He'll be livid, but you know what, that's something he'll have to live with now. This is the right thing to do, and the Hillderstaff legacy will not continue to be one of abuse of power or people."

Kevin Stone was writing frantically, trying to document every word. Shayna could feel Lincoln's body language growing tenser next to her.

"Don't do anything," she whispered. "Just trust me."

Two officers stood them up and removed the handcuffs. "You two will be escorted with your lawyers into a private conference room soon."

"Shayna, I wanted to let you know that your mother's removal from her clinical trial will be thoroughly investigated. As for your scholarships that were revoked without cause, I am sure we'll be able to get those reinstated. All of this will be corrected, and I, and any of my family who wants to make this right, will work with you to see how we can help not just you, but your community, going forward."

"Thank you," Shayna said brightly, throwing her arms dramatically around Nicholas. "I don't know how we could have done this without you. I know you'll help."

A camera shutter clicked behind her, and she knew right then things would be moving quickly. There would be no lag time between her trying to beg people to listen and getting actual help.

Nicholas had done something self-serving and slimy. He'd used the work she'd done, the risks she'd taken, and was now putting his name on it. Just another version of what her culture had been robbed of over and over again. But this time, it would drive change. It would bring some comfort. The outcome might not have been nearly as good had he not pulled this selfish garbage.

"Piper," Shayna said, leaning in and squeezing her hand, "call my brother and tell him the good news. Tell him Nicholas is going to make sure we get the help we need."

Someone led Shayna away, and she was flanked closely by a tall lawyer in a crisp business suit. "Everything is going to work out just fine now," he assured her firmly. "No one gets things done like a Hillderstaff."

"I know," Shayna sighed and rolled her eyes. "I wish I had thought of that sooner."

CHAPTER 28

Betty was about the only one who could make getting arrested funny. They all had shirts on with Shayna's mug shot and a cake with black and white stripes like an old time prison uniform. "Surprise," everyone yelled as Shayna walked into The Wise Owl Restaurant. It was loaded with black and white balloons and a big banner that said: "Welcome Home from the Clink." There were fake bars on the windows and upon closer inspection the cake had a big metal file baked into it.

"You guys are hilarious," Shayna said, tugging Lincoln in behind her. He looked downright terrified, and who could blame him.

"Come in, come in," Betty ordered, clearing the way so Shayna could get to her mother.

"You look good, Mom," Shayna said, so happy to see she'd gained some weight and had a little color back in her face.

"I'm trying to convince Betty she should turn this place into a recovery center. I've never had such good care or food in my life. Now I know why you liked coming here so much." Her mother reached up and pulled Shayna down for a kiss.

"I'm so sorry about all this, Mom. I didn't mean to keep you in the dark."

"I know, dear; your brother explained it all to me. I'm only sorry you had to deal with so much. Tell me the latest please."

"Well, unlike this party implies," Shayna laughed, "I haven't been in prison this whole time. I've actually been working with Nicholas, as strange as that sounds. The way he went about things was wrong, but he's certainly been an asset since then. They have a few forensic anthropologists working to identify bodies. They have twenty-two more former students willing to talk about what they experienced."

Frankie pulled her friend in for a hug and then pushed her back so she could see her expression. "It doesn't bother you at all that he's become the face of this whole thing? I saw him on nearly every national news channel. The ways he's talking, you'd think he put all of this together himself. That he single-handedly exposed the story."

"I couldn't care less," Shayna smiled brightly. "I'm back in school. My mother has the best care possible. Tao is actually considering enrolling in school out here. This story has gotten far more traction with Nicholas leading the way then it would have, had I been the face of it. I'm not losing a bit of sleep over it."

"And," Betty interrupted, tossing an arm over Lincoln's shoulder, "you found yourself a good man in prison."

Everyone broke out in laughter as Betty waived for her wait staff to start serving the food. "Don't forget our surprise guest," Piper said, parting the crowd to show Nurse Cybil blushing at all the attention.

"Cybil, you're here?" Shayna said, covering her mouth in surprise. "Have you been to the beach yet?"

"I was waiting," Cybil said, taking a plate of food that was handed to her.

"You've already waited so long," Shayna said, shaking her head in disbelief. "What were you waiting for?"

"You," Cybil explained. "I wouldn't be here if it wasn't for you."

"We'll go tomorrow," Shayna promised. "All of us."

Shayna's mother straightened up and tapped her daughter's arm. "Cybil has been giving me such good care. Everyone comes into our lives for a reason. You've been a magnet for love." She gestured around the room and Shayna couldn't argue with that.

"I'd like to make a toast," Michael said, raising his glass and quieting the room. "I think there are times in our lives where we all look for answers. We want to bring peace to ourselves and others. We spend a lot of time looking backward. And that's all right. Look at all Shayna was able to accomplish by unearthing the past. But at some point, we have to take stock and turn our sails toward the future. Now is that time. To making tomorrow matter as much as yesterday," Michael concluded.

"Cheers," everyone called out in unison as they tipped their drinks back.

"Thank you," Shayna said, hugging Michael tightly. She had grown up without her father. That had left her always wondering. Constantly longing. But that cloud of sadness had blocked her from seeing the people who had filled his absence. She lifted her glass and let her eyes glisten over with tears.

"To the family I found," Shayna said, choking on her words.

Betty cut in with a wide smile. "Do you think she's talking about us or the gang she joined in prison?"

"Oh, just drink," Shayna said, shaking her head and falling into Betty's open arms.

"Yes," Betty agreed, patting down Shayna's hair. "Drink. Eat. Laugh. Party. You never know when the cuffs will get slapped back on you. Okay, that was my last prison joke, I promise."

Lincoln stood in the corner of the restaurant, looking around like he might be ready to bolt.

"Hurry up," Shayna whispered to Betty. "Get that boy some pie. It's the only thing that might keep him from running."

Betty swatted Shayna's backside as she scurried off. "I can think of something else that might keep him around."

Shayna shot Lincoln a smile from across the room and mouthed an apology for the craziness. Betty was there a second later, spooning a bite of pie directly into his mouth. He began to protest until the flavors seem to burst to life, and his eyes went wide. She offered him the plate, and he happily took it from her. Betty gave her a wink and a thumbs up to let her know all was right in the world. Shayna shot a thumbs up back, and Betty knew the pie had done the trick. Lincoln wasn't going anywhere.

The End

ALSO BY DANIELLE STEWART

Piper Anderson Series:

Book 1: Chasing Justice

Book 2: Cutting Ties

Book 3: Changing Fate

Book 4: Finding Freedom

Book 5: Settling Scores

Book 6: Battling Destiny

Book 7: Unearthing Truth

Book 8: Defending Innocence

Piper Anderson Bonus Material:

Chris & Sydney Collection – Choosing Christmas & Saving Love

Betty's Journal - Bonus Material (suggested to be read after Book 4 to avoid spoilers)

Edenville Series – A Piper Anderson Spin Off:

Book 1: Flowers in the Snow

Book 2: Kiss in the Wind

Book 3: Stars in a Bottle

Book 4: Fire in the Heart

Piper Anderson Legacy Mystery Series:

Book 1: Three Seconds To Rush

Book 2: Just for a Heartbeat

Book 3: Not Just an Echo

The Clover Series:

Hearts of Clover - Novella & Book 2: (Half My Heart & Change My Heart)

Book 3: All My Heart

Over the Edge Series:

Book 1: Facing Home

Book 2: Crashing Down

Midnight Magic Series:

Amelia

Rough Waters Series:

Book 1: The Goodbye Storm

Book 2: The Runaway Storm

Book 3: The Rising Storm

Stand Alones:

Running From Shadows

Yours for the Taking

****

Multi-Author Series including books by Danielle Stewart

All are stand alone reads and can be enjoyed in any order.

Indigo Bay Series:

A multi-author sweet romance series

Sweet Dreams - Stacy Claflin

Sweet Matchmaker - Jean Oram

Sweet Sunrise - Kay Correll

Sweet Illusions - Jeanette Lewis

Sweet Regrets - Jennifer Peel

Sweet Rendezvous - Danielle Stewart

Short Holiday Stories in Indigo Bay:

A multi-author sweet romance series

Sweet Holiday Wishes - Melissa McClone

Sweet Holiday Surprise - Jean Oram

Sweet Holiday Memories - Kay Correll

Sweet Holiday Traditions - Danielle Stewart

Return to Christmas Falls Series:

A multi-author sweet romance series

Homecoming in Christmas Falls: Ciara Knight

Honeymoon for One in Christmas Falls: Jennifer Peel

Once Again in Christmas Falls: Becky Monson

Rumor has it in Christmas Falls: Melinda Curtis

Forever Yours in Christmas Falls: Susan Hatler

Love Notes in Christmas Falls: Beth Labonte

Finding the Truth in Christmas Falls: Danielle Stewart

****

BOOKS IN THE BARRINGTON BILLIONAIRE SYNCHRONIZED WORLD

By Ruth Cardello:

Always Mine

Stolen Kisses

Trade It All

Let It Burn

More Than Love

By Jeannette Winters:

One White Lie

Table For Two

You & Me Make Three

Virgin For The Fourth Time

His For Five Nights

After Six

Seven Guilty Pleasures

By Danielle Stewart:

Fierce Love

Wild Eyes

Crazy Nights

Loyal Hearts

Untamed Devotion

Stormy Attraction

Foolish Temptations

You can now download all Barrington Billionaire books by Danielle Stewart in a "Sweet" version. Enjoy the clean and wholesome version, same story without the spice. If you prefer the hotter version be sure to download the original. <u>The Sweet version still contains adult situations and relationships.</u>

Fierce Love - Sweet Version

Wild Eyes - Sweet Version

Crazy Nights - Sweet Version

Loyal Hearts - Sweet Version

Untamed Devotion - Sweet Version

Stormy Attraction - Sweet Version - Coming Soon

Foolish Temptations - Sweet Version - Coming Soon

NEWSLETTER SIGN-UP

If you'd like to stay up to date on the latest Danielle Stewart news visit www.authordaniellestewart.com and sign up for my newsletter.

One random newsletter subscriber will be chosen every month this year. The chosen subscriber will receive a $25 eGift Card! Sign up today.

AUTHOR CONTACT INFORMATION

Website: AuthorDanielleStewart.com
Email: AuthorDanielleStewart@Gmail.com
Facebook: facebook.com/AuthorDanielleStewart
Twitter: @DStewartAuthor